I0739057

The Book of Jacob

Jacob Grovey

Global Genius Society

 Austin, TX

GlobalGeniusSociety@gmail.com

www.GlobalGeniusSociety.com

Ordering Information:

Special discounts are available on quantity purchases by corporations, associations, and others. For details, contact the publisher at the address above.

Printed in the United States of America

This book is dedicated to the memory of my father, Gregory L. Grovey, Sr. Your legacy will forever be on my mind and the memories you left will forever be in my heart.

Jacob Grovey

Table Of Contents

I say it all of the time, everyone has a story to tell. Our life experiences have brought each one of us to where we are today. The things we were deprived of growing up will most certainly have an impact on what we hope to have in the future.

Unlike my last collection of poetry, "My World, My Words: Confessions of a Cluttered Mind," this collection is a bit more direct in its delivery. The poems that represent my past (and present) are true recollections of my emotions and thoughts during certain moments of my life (or the lives of those around me). But this isn't just about my past, or my present. This book also contains visions of the future. This collection is divided into sections based on the few cities I have had the pleasure to livein and what I was going through, feeling or thinking about during those times.

The failures of my previous days will constantly battle the triumphant times of days yet to come. This is both comedic and dramatic, it is sad and happy, fact and fiction. There are moments of extreme anger and moments of great joy. The following pages are how I recall my life combined with I how I hope certain aspects will turn out. Interspersed with the poems (and the city info) are details explaining why the poem was written, or what I was experiencing. As a result, you can either read this book cover to cover - as a single story, or skip around for the individual poems. Either way, I hope you are able to find a bit of inspiration in the pages that follow. Simply put, this is a portion of my life. This is "The Book of Jacob."

Houston:

This is my birthplace- this is where it all started. There's a certain aura in the city that seems to remain with you, no matter how long you remain there.

"(I was) birthed in the T-X and descended from the sky, unable to be perfect, but he gon' try" — Jacob (2010)

Being the first child of my family, I know the first born usually has a bit of extra pressure given to them before they have ever seen the light of day. As soon as the family learns there will be a new addition, their plans immediately start. The parents start thinking about college, a new place to live and even what they hope the child will be able to accomplish in their life. Sometimes the parents may even project their past hopes and dreams on their child. None of this is bad, per say, but it gives the child things they become responsible for even before day one.

I can't speak for you and say exactly how it was when you were birthed ... I can just say how I perceived it to be when I was born..

All of the first born children fall victim to this pressure, we all are statistics in some way....

<u>**When I Was Born**</u>

When I was born, they tried to play songs sung by the fat lady

Symbolic of hope dying before it starts, just like a typical black baby

Maybe it sounds crazy, but you can't say it ain't true

And if you do, it's probably because racism ain't been directed at you

Now, I was a stereo-type from day one, at least that's what they wanted

people to believe

I know many of them had thoughts of me failing at every single thing I

ever tried to achieve

Every once in a while they probably looked towards my mother's hospital room

and quietly shook their heads

Because when I cried as I began my life, they felt my dreams were already dead

But I am the first child of my parents and they have never given me the

option to lose

They looked out at the Houston streets and knew we all had something to prove

"An actual black family, nah they're not gonna make it"

So, we could either prove them right or show this world was ours for the takin'

Would we be able to stand up against adversity, or would we have to run?

To this day the answer is still unknown, but just think, this was just day one

When a baby is brought into the world, it seems everyone in the entire family (aunts, uncles, cousins, etc.) has expectations for that child. Everyone has opinions on how they feel the baby should look, dress, smell and how quickly they should reach certain milestones. I was no exception. Now, I'm sure whatever was said about me was done so out of love, but regardless of that, words can impact a person for years to come.

Our minds don't work the same. If they did, this would be a very boring world. Since this fact determines our foundation, we sometimes fail to realize people will not do all of the same things at the same time someone else did. I'm sure some people would have loved for me to start running around the very first day I was born, but of course that didn't happen.

Before we can run, we all have to take baby steps…

<u>Baby Steps</u>

I heard stories about how some family members used to think I was "slow"

I didn't walk when they expected me to because I simply had no place to go

Take a look @ my baby pictures, you can tell I was thinking

"Mom, Dad, could you come here? I think I smell my diaper stinking"

My cognitive cohesion was above where it should have been as a baby

'cause I thought, "Why walk when I can be carried?" That's just smart, I wasn't being lazy

"Now, you know you weren't thinkin' that. That ain't even true"

You can't assume you know what I was thinking. I wouldn't do that to you

But it's all good, I'm just a baby so I guess what I think doesn't matter

And maybe it's because I'm too young, but your words sometimes seem like nonsensical chatter

So, you can talk about my mental development now, but later on I bet it'll be something you will regret

One day I'll run the world, but for now, let me focus on making these baby steps

We all know life is unexpected from day one. Like I said, everyone has plans before a child is born, but then we usually realize we have to adapt to what's actually going on in the real world. Such was the case for my family. At the age of 3, we got to the point where it was just necessary to leave Houston. Being so young, of course I had absolutely no say in the matter, so I just had to deal.

Houston, we don't have a problem, but I think it's time I move on...

Movin' On

Well Houston, I think it's easy to see

You may work for some, but not for me

Blame it on me, it's certainly not you

All the wonderful things they say about you are most certainly true

Astroworld, the Astrodome, yeah the 713 was full of things that were fun

But at least for now, my time here is done

Maybe one day I'll visit, or maybe even stay

I just know at age 3, I must be on my way

No, no, Houston, please don't let any tears fall

Let's not hold any grudges, no, none at all

I'll still be in Texas, just a few hours away

Yeah, I'll be in Dallas... that's where I'm gonna stay

I know it didn't work out for us the way you wished it would

Don't be mad, Houston, it's still all good

I was born downtown, so I'll always be down

And you'll be in my heart, even when I'm not around

But this will be a new start for us, Houston, so no sad songs

This is "see you later," not "goodbye," 'cause for now I'm movin' on

Dallas:

We don't choose where we grow up. Even if we could, I don't know if I would have picked a place other than Dallas. I never grew up with the most material things, but the love my family provided made us feel like we were the richest people in the world.

I wasn't born in Dallas, but anyone who knows anything about me knows it is certainly where I grew up, where I started to learn who Jacob actually was. A lot of questions I had about life were first asked when I was growing up there. The first time I wondered what life really was happened in Dallas.

Oak Cliff (the area of Dallas where I spent most of my years) made me question many things about my surroundings.

Sometimes, I had to literally look at the person in the mirror and ask what was going on…

Reflections

As a young kid, I'd look in the mirror sometimes as soon as I would wake up

Looking at my parents, I'd ask who's that, they'd reply "That's Jacob."

At first I couldn't really understand the concept of reflections

There just seemed to be a cool little dude staring back in my direction

It took me a little while to understand that cool little dude was actually me

And in the mirror, it was Jacob Grovey who I would be able to see

At first I would always go and see when I had a smile on my face,

showing my teeth

I thought this mirror stuff was cool, because it only showed glee

But then I learned it also showed me how I looked when I was sad

It reflected back the good times, but also when the times were bad

This is when I started to realize the sort of things I didn't like

In my simple way, I just asked my folks, "So, this is life?"

Believe it or not, seeing the reflection helped me realize

You can tell how a person was feeling by looking into their eyes

When I was mad, my eyes showed it, for other emotions this was true as well

I noticed how sometimes when we were happy and laughing, our eyes would

close, when we were sad they would swell

Again, I was young, so there was a lot I didn't know

But learning to read the reflections would help my mentality grow

So, I practiced with everyone, my family and even those at school

I could learn how to tell when people were scared, or when they felt "cool"

When I saw how they felt, it helped me know how I would act

I may have wanted to be a certain way, but then I'd retract

It helped me be a better person, at least at that age that's what I thought

Who would have thought these would be the types of lessons a simple

mirror taught?

I started to see the world didn't always have it as good as me.. some people only

knew pain

And even though I was still a kid, I started to see that Michael was right when he

said the man in the mirror had to make a change

So, I tried to make one, even without really knowing what I was doing

I just wanted everyone to be happy, well, at least that's what I was pursuing

So, to this day...I admit I haven't reached that goal, these words can serve as a

confession

I just know it all started a long time ago by simply seeing my reflection

A major part of life, especially when you're young, is education. Of course our first teachers are our families, but we all have those teachers who had a great impact. I'm speaking about the teachers who, for whatever reason, become our favorites. For me, that teacher was my 3rd grade instructor, Mrs. Armstrong.

Mrs. Armstrong was like one of those teachers you'd see on television. She had a unique style of instructing that made learning fun. It felt like we were playing all day, but when the final bell rang, we realized we all had a lot of information in our heads we didn't have when the day started. I have always admired teachers and how much they sacrifice to educate others.

To Mrs. Armstrong and those like her, I say "Teach on..."

<u>Teach On</u>

Teaching has to be one of the most underrated and under appreciated professions

in America

The future leaders of this country are left in their care everyday, yet many people

look at them as if their jobs are insignificant

It's nothing to see an athlete get paid $20 million a season, or an actor get paid

that much per film, but teachers....well, we'd be beyond surprised if we see one of

them making $70,000

So, that shows how little value we actually place on education

In spite of that, I still am amazed

Amazed at how many people in this country still strive to be teachers

They know how important it is to teach

How impressionable students are and how necessary it is to be a positive role

model in their lives

One such teacher came into my world in the 3rd grade

Her name was Mrs. Armstrong

Admittedly, I don't really think I cared too much for her or her class at first

She wasn't one of those teachers that accepted when one of her students said "I

can't..."

She believed in us more than we believed in ourselves

She held us to a very high standard and she wouldn't let go until we all reached

the highest point we possible could

Soon, my feelings towards my 3rd grade class were the complete opposite of where they started off

I enjoyed going to class

I enjoyed the challenge

….I was thankful for my teacher

She was like a show all of us would watch on television

She was entertaining, but we always learned

We all knew we would only be around her for a certain amount of time everyday

Yet it always seemed like time went by too quickly

In addition to my parents, Mrs. Armstrong became one of the reasons I had to

maintain high grades

I just couldn't let any of them down

Over the years, I heard some things had taken her teaching career off course

That saddened me

Knowing my teacher, though, I knew she would still find a way to teach

So this is just a thank you letter, of sorts, to her

It doesn't matter if you're in a class or not, Mrs. Armstrong…

I thank you and just ask that you teach on

As the years passed, I continued to discover new things about life. One of the simple things I learned early on was music made me happy. I got into music early because my father always played all sorts of music, so I liked some of everything. Most 10-year-olds I knew didn't like jazz, funk, r&b, blues and all sorts of other music, but I wasn't (and still am not) like most people.

My parents loved music, especially my father. So, when I had the chance to actually learn how to play music on my own, I was super excited. Now, I can't remember the exact date, but I do remember it was a day that changed my life. Mr. Adkins was my first band teacher…

…and I have to thank him for helping Jacob become "The Trumpeter."

The Trumpeter

Even before I knew why I liked certain instruments and sounds, there were two

that really stuck out to me

Sure, I loved the way the drums truly provided the rhythm for a song, but that

wasn't one of the ones for me

The piano....well nobody can deny its importance, but that didn't really

do it for me either

The bass, while it was cool, that wasn't one of the instruments I gravitated

towards, either

No, the two that were special to me were the saxophone and the trumpet

The saxophone was smooth

It was like one of the cool kids in class that everyone else one wanted to be like

Well, everyone except for the trumpet

The trumpet was cool on its own

It seemed to have a certain kind of energy that went along with it

It was almost like the trumpet forced you to be happy, no matter

how you actually felt

They were both like drugs that just made you feel different

One day, I had to choose between the two

How was I supposed to do that, though?

I knew neither one of them, but I cared for them both

My band teacher allowed me to play them to see if my ability seemed better on

one than it was on the other

That didn't help

Playing both seemed natural

Which was strange, but at the same time it wasn't surprising

Not trying to toot my own horn (pardon the pun), but music was a part of my life

Yes, it was true I had never played any instrument

But it seemed the ability to play was passed down to me from my father, like so

many other of his personality traits

I was now feeling a bit of pressure

Do I go with the energy instrument, or the one that's known for being cool?

Yeah, I knew they were both inanimate objects, but I still felt I would hurt the

feelings of the one that was not chosen

I thought carefully

I tried to play both again

There was something about the trumpet

It seemed simple, even though it was complex

I felt it was like me

Then I thought some more

The saxophone seemed a bit pretentious

Did I want to play that?

Did I want to seem that way?

Did I want to play the cool instrument to be cool?

Absolutely not!

Who was I trying to kid?

At that point, no matter what you played, a "band geek" was still what I

would be called

That was not a problem

So, my decision was made

I was going to play the trumpet

I was about to start my life as a trumpeter

Learning to play the trumpet provided me with a little bit more confidence in myself. However, I soon learned going through those "awkward years" of life can make you lose any confidence you have. That certainly was the case for me. Sure, I had some things going for me and I felt my life was pretty cool, I soon learned others didn't always have a positive outlook on who I was.

Somewhere around the age of 12, it became evident I was no longer in the age of my peers being friendly all of the time. I had gotten to the point where some people seemingly made it their only objective to make others feel bad. This is when it became common place for people to call me fat, short or four eyes. It wasn't that any of these descriptions were off, I just wasn't able to hear people telling me the truth, I guess.

This is where my shyness and insecurities became a big issue, bigger than they ever were before…

Growing Pains

Umm, is it necessary to actually grow to be going through growing pains?

Such was one of the many questions I was asking prior to those teenage years

Everybody was getting taller

But not me

Everybody was talking about how confident they were

How they felt they could do anything

Somehow, those feelings didn't come my way

That's when I really started to learn about growing pains

See the pain of growing was hitting me

Everyday I went to school, someone felt it was their duty to remind me...

Remind me that I was short

Remind me that I was still carrying what some family members called

"baby weight"

I was hurt

Not physically

No, nobody ever tried to bully me because I always had friends who would look

out for me

Emotionally, though, I had to fend for myself

People found it to be extremely hilarious to talk bad about me

They swore they were the first to call me "shorty"

They thought they owned a trademark on the word "shrimp"

Added to that, was the fact I wore glasses

So, "What's up four eyes?" was something I heard daily

I vividly remember telling them "I have two eyes and a pair of glasses...idiot!"

Smart-mouthed responses may have upset them a little, but it made them leave

me alone

At least for a moment

Let's not forget... I played the trumpet as well

Everyone knew I enjoyed playing music

I enjoyed being in band

But it wasn't "cool"

So, this was yet another verbal bullet people liked to shoot off at me

I not only had low self esteem because of it all, sometimes I hated myself

I wondered why I was a short, glasses-wearing, band geek

Then I realized something

I wasn't the one with the problem

They were

Nobody had the right to talk bad about me

Nobody should have been given the power to make me feel bad about myself

So, why did I allow it?

It was allowed simply because I didn't know any better

But once I learned

The pain of growing seemed a lot less painful

It seemed like...well, like maybe getting older wouldn't be so bad

Even if others tried to make sure they let me know why they thought they were

better than me

It was during this time that I realized something

In spite of what "they" thought...

I was awesome

And I thank the growing pains for letting me know

So, life continued. I found when you're a child, you swear you know everything there is to know about the world. As you get older, you convince yourself you absolutely know your opinion on everything is right and those who disagree are not only wrong, but they have to be crazy! We all go through this phase at some point. It's not something our parents look forward to, but they know to expect it because they did the same thing.

As a senior in high school, I had really started to settle into my personality. I was quiet when I didn't know you, and perhaps I talked a bit too much once I did. I was sometimes stubborn, and I seemed to always have a sly remark ready to shoot off at anyone who I felt deserved it. Another thing that was going on at that time, I certainly started to think I was grown.

In my parents' minds, being grown meant handling things on your own - including things such as rent, phone bills, utilities bills, etc. And since I was living at home with them and not paying for any of those things, they quickly told me I was not grown. I guess to not make me feel bad, they reminded me that I was about to go off to school, and since that was the case, they would say I was almost grown.

Now "almost" grown was nothing more than a frivolous title they gave to me, but I accepted it because if nothing else, it sounded better than just being a kid.

"Almost" Grown

The world and everyone around me is changing

We are all getting older

My friends are starting to tell me about how they have more responsibilities

How they have to do more

But not me

It seems like I'm still just a child

My little brother is getting older, but it's difficult to discern the age difference

At least from the outside

I mean, what am I "allowed" to do that he isn't?

Can I stay out with no curfew?

Nope, but would I want to even if I could?

Maybe not

Perhaps my personality isn't the going out type

Wait, what is my personality?

You would think if I want to be considered grown, I could at least know how my personality is

Maybe that's why my parents still looked at me as a child

It is my fault because I haven't started to actually "get" what life is

So, if that's the case... do all of my friends already have it together?

Do their parents see something in them mine don't see in me?

Am I over thinking things?

I have a habit of doing that, so that wouldn't surprise me

Wait, have I even asked for more responsibilities?

Have I asked to be treated like I'm grown?

They say "a closed mouth don't get fed"

How true that statement is

My desire for being treated differently by my family can't be granted if I never

speak on it

So, finally I do

I ask to get a job

The next thing I knew, I was working

I asked for a car

The next thing I knew, I was driving

My level of responsibilities grew simply by asking

I learned I had to speak up sometimes

People aren't mind readers no matter how obvious you think your non-verbal

signs are

After getting just about everything I wanted, there was one other thing I

needed to request

That was... to simply be treated like I was grown

At 17, I don't even remember what my idea of "being treated like I was grown"

meant...

I just knew that's what I wanted

So, that's what I asked for

My parents... they have always had a good sense of humor, so they asked me

what I meant

They laughed as I tried to fake my way through an explanation

"So, you want to be grown, huh?"

I was sure I did, so I said yes

"So, you're ready to help out with utilities and rent, right? I know you're ready to chip in when we go to the grocery store, right?"

I had to quickly rethink this "grown" thing

"Umm... I don't think I'm really ready for all of that."

"Well, son, that's some of what grown folks have to deal with."

I understood.... I even agreed.... but that didn't mean I liked it

"Look, we know what it's like to be your age

You're old enough to feel grown, but young enough to not really be treated

that way"

They were right

But they knew that

"I'll tell you what...we know we still treat you like a child, but we shouldn't

You haven't ever led us to believe you are irresponsible

However, you are not grown."

I thought we were making progress, but that certainly didn't make me feel like it

"Let me just say this, we know you are about to graduate.

We know that means you are about to leave home.

So, we know things are different, but you still don't pay for anything....yet.

So, how about for your last year here, we say you're almost grown

And when you leave, we'll drop the world almost."

What would the new title bring?

Would that actually make things different in life?

Would I be expected to know more information immediately?

Then I thought about it

Grown people are supposed to know things

They are supposed to be the ones to have things figured out

"Almost grown" people....

Well, I think we are given the freedom to just figure things out along the way

And if that's the case....

Maybe I shouldn't be in a rush to be grown after all

Tallahassee:

There comes a point in every person's life where they must leave the comfort of "home." For me, this time came after I graduated high school and moved to Tallahassee, Florida to attend Florida A&M University.

Some people know exactly what to expect when they go off to school. They were able to read all of the literature about the school and what it's like to be on campus. Some people were even fortunate enough to take tours of their school so they can see everything for themselves. You also have many whose family members found a school they liked and everyone else just followed tradition. My situation did not fit into those categories.

When I first heard about Florida A&M, there was something about it I liked. I had never been there, and nobody in my family had gone there. I knew it was in Tallahassee, FL, but I knew absolutely nothing about the city. When I started to tell my family that's where I wanted to go, I was simply asked, "Why?"

I couldn't really answer their question. All I could do was say that in my heart, I felt that's where I needed to go. That's where the next part of my life needed to take place. So, being supportive parents, they allowed me to fly far away from the nest.

So I could learn to soar on my own, they gave me the ability to be a free bird...

Free Bird

The nest had become comfortable

So comfortable, in fact, I almost felt...bored

I had everything I needed

But yet I felt restrained

I had all the support in the world

But I felt I had to go

I was able to fly close to the nest

I just reached a point where I wanted to see what was beyond that nest

I wanted to be able to fly through clouds I wasn't used to seeing

So, when I saw everyone I grew up with flocking together to leave

I found myself flying alone

Was I nervous?

Not really because I felt it was what I was supposed to do

So, as my parents watched...

I flew

I flew away from Dallas...

To a place where I had no family and I knew very few people

This was my first chance to see who I really was

It was time to see what being free was all about

No matter when you leave home, no matter how much fun you're having, there will come a time when you will think about it. College not only gave me a time to enjoy a new environment and learn, it also gave me time to reflect about growing up in Dallas. People have their views of the major cities in this country, even if they've never been anywhere near them. Dallas is no exception.

Places are just reflections of the people who live there. As such, it's easy to understand a place cannot be all positive, just as it can't be all negative. My hometown certainly has it's share of negativity surrounding it. One day, I just happened to be thinking about that. It made me get into the mindset of the people who live in neighborhoods worse than the ones I grew up in. I thought back to various news stories I saw about corruption and death. I became both angry and sad.

What was written were not just my own feelings, but the feelings of others...

Straight Path

The straight path I was on has led me astray

God why'd you lead me this way?

I try to walk how you would if you were here on earth

But doing good seems to be a good way to get hurt

A stray bullet hits another kid on the block

Yet another case turned away by the cops

Everyday seems like a repeat on the TV

Living my life wondering if anybody sees me

Second thought, maybe I'll remain unknown

Maybe it's how I made it this long

Back in the day, things never seemed to be this way

As long as you were with your people, you always felt safe

But the same people who used to show positive affection

Are the ones pointing their heads in the opposite direction

For years I've been able to picture my coffin

Now days it seems that happens way too often

The straight path I was on has led me astray

God why'd you lead me this way?

I try to walk how you would if you were here on earth

But doing good seems to be a good way to get hurt

Don't get it twisted, I love where I grew up dearly

But over the crime, growing up, I wondered if God could even hear me

The spiritual leaders who used to live in my hood

Are now the main ones who are up to no good

God used to be their main objective, it was their number 1

But dime bags became more important than the 'building fund'

Used to run prayers, but now you see them runnin' numbers

Wanted a mansion in the sky, but the alley's where folks now slumber

Got me takin' off my glasses, 'cause that ain't what I wanna see

The devil won with you, but he ain't gonna win with me

It doesn't matter what you do, or what you say

I ain't gonna allow myself to even think of going out that way

I try to always keep my head up high

When most folks just give up and wonder why

I can't even answer if you still gotta ask

I'm tryin' to pass the detours to stay on the right path

The straight path I was on has led me astray

God why'd you lead me this way?

I try to walk how you would if you were here on earth

But doing good seems to be a good way to get hurt

Another thing about college- in addition to thinking about how you grew up and where you're from, you start realizing people are immediately put into different types of situations. Some people, no matter how far or close they are from home, still have full support of their families. People like that don't have to worry about anything because their families are paying for their tuition, food, books and everything else they want or need. I don't really know if this is the norm, though.

For many, once a child goes off to school, they start to struggle on their own. Most of the time, this is not because their family doesn't want to help them, it's simply because they aren't financially able. Books can cost hundreds of dollars, that alone could put a strain into anybody's budget.

With that being said, some students quickly go into survival mode. They feel if they want to make it in this world, they have to do whatever they see fit to try to accomplish their goals. Their decisions may not be seen as good ones from everyone else's perspective, but people outside of those particular situations don't know what that life can be like. Sometimes the things learned up to that point are (at least temporarily) thrown out of the window.

The following is the start of the story of someone who was made to survive.

She is just trying to make it in this world, and her story needs to be told...

Stripped to the Soul (1/3 of her journey)

With every layer of clothing she stripped off, she seemed to put on another layer of
her insecurities
She moved on stage as if she were trying to move away from herself...
From who she really was
But she was now a woman who really had no idea of who she was
She used to, though
She looked off of that stage into the eyes of all of the men who were staring @ her
She unrealistically searched for the look of hope
The look of faith
The look of salvation
Instead, she just saw judgment
The same look of judgment she always seemed to get from her family when she
was younger
The one that usually combined with disappointment
And together, those two formed a supernatural force that could easily rip apart
anything that stood in their way
Did she want to do what she was doing?
Of course not, but when you are trying to pay your own way through school
because your parents have pretty much disowned you, what options
are you left with?
Sadly, the options were very few
She never thought she would be getting undressed for strangers

That was not her personality

Outside of work, she was a shy individual

Generally, she was quiet except for when she felt she needed to express herself

Every night she danced, she felt she died a little

This was a terrible way to be, especially for someone who was so young

One night, when she was supposed to be off, she was called in to see if she

wanted to make some extra money

The truth of the matter was, she had no to desire to go to work, but being a

struggling student, she couldn't really turn down the money

She had a bad feeling in the pit of her stomach, but she fought that and

went anyway

She kept a fake smile on her face as she danced for her tips

A few hours into the night, she had a customer who wanted a private dance

She always hated those

It made her feel unsafe

But on the other hand, she always got a lot of money

The guy who wanted a private dance that night was not like her usual customers

He was dressed in a tailored suit and he didn't have an entourage of people with him

"Okay, quit worrying so much"

She tried to convince herself it was all good

She thought she saw the man slide the bouncer outside of the room some money,

but then she told herself she didn't

The music was blasting loudly as she went into the room

It seemed a little louder than normal

Something was different

She went over to the guy

He sat back and smiled

There was nobody in the room with them, but she had to pretend she was okay

Her customer was enjoying his individualized attention

The money was quickly leaving his hands and she loved that

Soon, he started to touch her, though

"Now you know you can't do that! Just play nice!"

She tried to tell him the rules, but he already knew them

He just didn't care

Her heart was pounding

She was scared, but she wanted the money

So, she disregarded her better judgment

She shouldn't have, though

Soon he was touching her more…

Which turned into grabbing….

Soon, she was so scared she was yelling out to the man on the outside of the

room…

He was supposed to protect her…

He didn't, though

He pretended not to hear

Soon, the lights went out as her screams got louder

The music seemed to go up as well, so nobody beyond the bouncer could hear

She couldn't believe what was happening to her

That voice inside told her not to go to work

But the money kept calling

Now, she's calling…

Calling for help…

Please, somebody answer the call…

(to be continued)

So, college is when you're supposed to start to learn who you really are. You're supposed to see your true character because you're not around your parents. Well, what I found was that who I was at home was pretty much who I had always been. However, I found that I no longer just accepted things. I found it was necessary to observe more and ask more questions. When doing so, I found that a big question that was around was, "What's it like to be a young, black person in this day and age?" Well, that's a loaded question? Since "being young" is actually subjective, I can't really say what it's like. However, the other part of that question, the one about being a black person, that's something different.

See, being black is both good and bad. Now, before I start getting people upset with me and start saying I'm one of those "self-hating" black people who wishes I was something else, remain calm. That's not me at all. I don't want to be anything other than what I am, but I try to base my thoughts and opinions off of logic and reality with a little bit of emotion sprinkled in.

Being black is good because, no matter what the situation is, you know for a fact there are people who look and sound like you who have made it out of things that were much worse. It lets you know we come from survivors; therefore, we can also survive. Also, you can't help but smile when you see people of different ethnic groups trying to speak or act the way that we commonly do. It gives you a sense of pride about your people and what you are a part of.

On the other hand, because we have a history deeply rooted in struggle, we all seem to have a very unhealthy fear of going back. If one of us "makes it," we seem to want to dismiss them and their accomplishments. On the radar of our many collective problems is the use of the so-called "n-word."

As a people, we have evolved... The real question is, how much?

The Nggr Evolution

"Nggr, get off the ship, zip your lip & hurry up and get to work

Or feel this whip and the hurt of not having any worth

Say goodbye to your family, 'cause you ain't gonna see them again

Wave goodbye to your dreams, this is where they end

I am your master, in both mind and soul

And you can forget about your gold and all of your regal clothes

See, your life ain't nothin', you're just property that I own

You mean less to me than all of the crops that I've grown

You women might as well smile, 'cause ain't no point of crying

I would tell you everything will be okay, but I ain't one for lying

Little kids, don't be like the others, just do what I say

And only then may you live to see another day"

This is how it started, doomsday and groundhog's day combined

Misery loves company, so she became best friend with time

Time didn't stay still, it didn't wait for a new year to have a resolution

Let's move forward in the story of The Nggr Evolution

"Nggr get to the back of the bus, you know this ain't where you belong

You better move quick and get happy by singing one of those old negro songs

Don't y'all talk about how all y'all gonna overcome?

Well I don't understand, 'cause it seems like your life is over...done!"

He stood up and laughed, pushed us to the back like trash

We had to give up our seats as we watched the white folks walk past

It was sad, we knew we had a difficult fight on our hands

We hated dealing with the devil, but we knew how he liked to dance

So we sang the songs they all wanted to hear

Called them boss, sir and ma'am, but in our mind, it was already clear

We really wanted peace, but we were ready for a fight

So we worked together until even the darkness saw the light

That was the second stage of The Nggr Evolution

The part where we showed unity and were ready for a revolution

Something had to give, or something was gonna break

It was time for things to change, we took all we were gonna take

We wanted something other than that life, even if it meant death

We were gonna try to get right until we had nothing left

"What's up Ngga?" Oh, I see we put an "a" where there used to be an "r"

I guess that means we've made progress, I guess we've come really far

"Say, ngga, yo' whip ain't fckn wit' mine"

Many times I'm confused if we're in the present, or if we've gone back in time

In this day and age, all we have to do is search to find success, but we don't even
want to look

They can tell us all of the world's riches are in the library and we still won't pick
up a book

What a shame. I don't even know who's to blame

'Cause if history was any different, would we still be the same?

How many years has it been since Lincoln let us go?

Does progress always take its time, or is it just us moving slow?

I guess we thought with new leaders our problems would stop

But if we all have a "crab in the bucket" mentality, how are any of us supposed to reach the top?

So, The Nggr Evolution has brought us right to where we are
We still are connected to chains and we'll sell our souls for soles and cars
They don't have to tell us go to the back, we do that on our own

It seems we couldn't call anyone who cares, even if they gave us a phone
Now hold on! We gettin' killed by the cops, but more of us are gettin' killed by civilians in our 'hoods
We smile with our gold teeth as we try to convince ourselves it's all good
Well, is it? If this is all good, I don't ever want to see bad
We already have way more than the ancestors of the past ever had
But we also have problems they never would have dreamed
I guess that's how it is, when it's all about c.r.e.a.m.
Is the Nggr gonna evolve or just destined to die slow?
If you accept the term Nggr, I think you already know...

And sure, there are many problems surrounding the black community, but problems and black people are not mutually exclusive. Everyone has problems. Many of us are overly opinionated and judgmental. The irony of that statement is that I'm being both opinionated and judgmental by saying it, and I certainly understand that.

Sometimes, we have to embrace the irony. Sometimes we may have to go outside of our normal character. I step away from the calm, mild mannered Jacob who writes and I become a slightly more vocal individual who raps. When such is the case, my opinion is a bit more direct.

When I get tired of certain things, I will speak on them...

<u>(untitled)</u>

It seems that today people fall in lust with lies

They turn into lemmings leaping into lackluster wordplay from losers

Lames act as if its law to lure lineage with lines of luxury...

Like lingering on corners with illegal items is the first and last way to live large

If I live less than lavishly, should I not be loved?

Should I not be respected 'cause I ain't a thug?

Should lies leave my lips as I portray a reality I'm not capable of?

Do lyrics mean nothing and those that deliver them mean even less?

Should I allow nonsense to get me upset?

I digress

Heres what i will do...

I'll temporarily leave my jovial life and learn to live with the likes of you

See, we all learn life lessons from everyone we are around

Even when it seems you are a part of a circus because you only seem to gravitate

towards clowns

Well, here's how it's going down

I will not limit my lines to tales about drug sales and coming up with an alibi

It should be no surprise I won't fail or compromise

I'll let loose wordplay that will be viewed by most as nonlinear

Rappers and "urban writers" seem to get fatter pockets when their subject matter

becomes skinnier

Well look, listen and learn the truth

Jacob Grovey is almost allergic to lies and my words are the proof

It would behoove anyone who sees or hears my writing, and or my name

To allow me to stay in my lane cause you're wasting time trying to get me to

change

See the ideas in my brain are the ones that I try to pursue

I do what I want, I'm not concerned with being cool

As a matter of fact, I'm not concerned with you

I'm not concerned with your words, raps, cars, money or anything you do

In leu of being a sell out writing duplicator

I'll think outside of the normally confining industry to be an originator

And soon the herds of people that currently follow your words and sounds

Will become squares because they'll no longer be around

I repeat... the herds of people that currently follow your words and sound

Will become squares because they'll no longer be around

No matter how much we talk about ourselves, revolutions, making our communities better, not following trends and trying to be unique, we still all like to be fashionable. Nobody is immune to this. No matter what your personal style is, you want your outer appearance to match how you're feeling inside. Part of the completion of the outside appearance is your shoes.

A long time ago, us guys weren't really concerned with shoes. We might just rock a pair of all blacks or all whites and that would be sufficient. Things are different now, though. If we feel bright and energetic, our shoes will match that. If we have a new shirt or hat that we want to stand out, we will make sure our shoes help out with that, but the new love for shoes isn't always just about the shoes themselves. Sometimes it's about the memories associated with them (good or bad).

So, could you walk a mile in these shoes?

<u>These Shoes</u>

I'm as fly as these J's, a symbolic Air Force of 1

If I can't do it, then it simply can't be done

You see the soles on these shoes? They're as translucent as my intentions

I see through your lies, I think I may need an intervention...

For all of the miles you have claimed to walk, my shoes actually hold proof

You use hyperbole with others, but I know what's made up and what's the truth

You say you run the game, but you must be running to lose

I guarantee you can't run nothin', at least not in these shoes

If we're evaluating our own journey, or walking a mile in someone else's shoes, it won't take long before we realize there is usually some type of movement taking place. If you really think about it, we are making moves more often than we give ourselves credit for. We dismiss our progress because we think our forward movement is far too minuscule to actually count it as doing anything. I do this all of the time.

I have always had a habit of setting goals, but thinking they were so far away from where I actually was, I would start to get upset. I would question if I was being realistic, or if I was just wasting time even believing I could achieve certain things. I would see people becoming famous for pursuing their passions and thinking they were "lucky." Sure, luck may have had a little to do with their success, but the truth of the matter is, most people who are successful simply work extremely hard. They don't give up when times are difficult. No, they tend to use those times for motivation.

It is sometimes difficult for me to realize how far faith and determination can take you.

Not only are my problems of yesterday a day away, but my prosperity could be a day away as well...

One Day Away

You could be one day away from composing the world's greatest song

A short journey away from starting to right all of your wrongs

24 hours from making someone smile

Or 1440 minutes away from walking your last mile

1 day may separate you from rediscovering God

And finding out that the devil is nothing more than a fraud

You can be right around the corner from buying your first home

Or finding you've reached the last day of you ever being alone

Tomorrow could be the day you get the degree from school that nobody in your

family ever has

You can immediately see the dream come true of both your mom and your dad

The day after today can show you how far you've come, but how far you still have

to go

It can be the day you realize the things you thought you knew, are really the things

you don't know

You may have been depressed for a while, but when the sun rises, that could

change

And the feeling of happiness can make depression seem foreign and strange

See, a lot can change quickly, like in 24 hours or less

A day can bring you a wife, or a child, or just alleviate your stress

A new day can help you gain appreciation for what it is you have

It can help you move beyond what you lost, or what you never had

In 24 hours, a young preacher can tell the world his dream

He can tell everyone about his vision of the future, no matter how bad the present

may seem

We can put our mark on this world, leave a legacy that let it be known we truly

had something to say

In spite of what's going on right now, keep faith and optimism, for you may just be

one day away

Riverside:

When you're pursuing your dreams, every now and again, you will have to take a leap of faith. For me, moving to Riverside, California was just that. Going to a new place can be scary, but when you are doing what you feel you are supposed to be doing with your life, fear doesn't really come into play. Well, with me it didn't.

When you move to a new city, sometimes you are so caught up with your new environment, you let things right in front of your eyes mess you up. You pay too much attention to things you shouldn't and not enough to things you should. At some point, there will be an emotion that will make you look and feel totally ignorant. For me, love happens to be that emotion.

I don't know about anyone else, but just when I think I fully understand the concept of what love is, I'm proven to be wrong. See, when things go right, love will make you get the warm feeling inside.

When it blindsides you, it is nothing more than an intruder...

<u>Intruder</u>

I thought my emotional security system was pretty strong

I assured myself I had invested enough into it to never be worried

That all changed when I saw her

The exact moment our eyes met, it was like she already was working on getting

all of my access codes

The one to my past

The codes to access my hopes and dreams

Or maybe she'll just go for the master code: the one to my heart

That's what the last one did

Actually, it was because of the last one that I had to step up my defense system

I pretty much gave her all access and before I knew it, I had to reevaluate my

emotional status

I had to take a step back and think about all of the decisions that had lead me to

that point

And after I did that, I still had to deal with the fact my 'home' was an absolute wreck

My thoughts were scattered everywhere

She caused me to feel as if I had gone through it all before

As if she was not the first to rob me of love only to leave behind a broken heart

I couldn't file a police report because that wouldn't do any good

Instead, I just had to rebuild everything

Just as I had done in the past

And like I would probably have to do in the future

I wished there was some way I could ensure my domestic tranquility

But no company in the world would guarantee anything like that

So, what am I supposed to do?

Am I supposed to wait for another home invasion?

Do I need to wear a cupid-proof vest to try and protect my heart from being

wounded again?

No, because avoiding pain is almost like voiding your emotional contract

And trust me, none of us can afford for that to happen

At some point the homes to our emotions will be invaded

We can't avoid it

All we can do is hope, at some point, we get out of the neighborhood of intruders

and move to where there are only invited guests

Anyone who has ever spent a few minutes talking with me can usually tell what kind of person I am. They can tell that I love the idea of love, I like to laugh and they can tell I'm initially shy. They can tell I am willing to debate about my opinion, but most will also say that I'm generally a calm person.

I try not to get loud when I'm speaking and I try to respect those people I'm speaking with. As a matter of fact, I don't even use curse words when I'm speaking. But sometimes, even the calmest person will have to vent. Sometimes things will touch a nerve and you are seemingly forced to speak on it.

Not long after moving to Riverside, a lot of thoughts started to cross my mind. I became a bit upset. I wasn't really upset at anyone in particular (at least not that I can recall now), but I felt many things were not the way I would have liked for them to be.

I had to vent, so I did so through my writing...

<u>Fck U</u>

Fck u

Fck u to those women I wasn't good enough for

Using my heart and emotions as a springboard that helped you jump to your next

relationship

Fck those 'family' members who are against me...those that are against my family

Looking @ us; wearing imaginary robes, carrying imaginary gavels

Judging us as you look down your nose

You are not better than us

Nor will you ever be

Fck my so-called friends who told me not to follow my dreams

Those who didn't support me trying to reach a state of constant happiness

While we are on the subject of my dreams, fck the entertainment industry I, and

so many others are trying to become a part of

Fck the record and studio executives who think they know what the world wants

to see and hear

It is because of them, creativity lies stagnant as the works of brilliant minds are

thrown into the garbage

Sitting there not getting a chance to live

Fck the people who want to censor the artist's vision

Fck a ratings board giving something an R-rating because of sex, but someone

getting killed violently is deemed okay to be shown to 13 year olds

Fck parental advisory stickers on music

How about advisory stickers against those who shouldn't be parents

Speaking of which, fck the so called 'man' who is macho enough to sleep with a

girl, but quickly turns into a btch if she gets pregnant

Take some fckin' responsibility for your actions

It's because of you, women don't believe decent guys such as myself even exist

And although I am by no means a fan of abortion, fck those who want to take

away a woman's right to do so

It's HER body!

Fck those in control whose sole objective is to have things done their way

Putting money in their pockets and away from those who deserve it

Fck those responsible for the current state of social security

It is because of you, good people like my grandparents had to keep working even

after 'retirement'

And when they died, people had to hustle to find a way to give them a proper

funeral and burial

In general, fck anyone who is trying to make someone feel unworthy of being

happy

That excludes no one

Fck me whenever I get down on myself for some stupid reason

Whenever I don't trust myself or my judgment

Fck the thoughts of crying I had while I was writing this

Fck the memories of 'good' people in my past who turned out to be undercover

a-holes

And if I offended anyone, there are no apologies because it was meant for you

And I pray you're removed from my life so there won't be a need for a Fck U (part II)

Okay, so the last poem may have been a little unexpected. That's understandable. I mean, sometimes we all get so angry we just feel like yelling loudly. Well, since my voice tends to start hurting immediately after I yell, and the fact that when I speak I don't use curse words, I tend to just write my venting moments down on paper. It allows me to not only clear my head and feel better, but it also gives me written evidence of how I was feeling at that point in my life.

I try not to hold onto the negative things too long, but I fail miserably with that a lot of the times. It's something I know and I always try to work on, but the process can be difficult. When such happens, I usually find myself thinking about time. Time is a strange thing. Depending on how you feel, it can seem as if time is literally flying by, or it can seem as if it's dragging on. It's a very strange thing, indeed.

No matter how time may feel like it's moving, it's still moving. There are many times when I wish I could freeze moments of joy, but of course this is impossible. There are other times when I wish I could just fast forward through all of the moments that are hurting me.

Sometimes, I wish the life clock had no hands...

<u>**Clock With No Hands**</u>

Like clock work, the clock works against me

The paranoia buried in my heart has taken the place of the second hand

The hours seem to move in slow motion, ensuring I will feel the pain

But @ the same time, I continuously lose track of time

I can't get past the sounds of the tick-tocks that seem to flip flop between

happiness and misery

It keeps giving me time to be alone

But do I actually want to be alone?

It doesn't matter

As more time passes, I realize less time remains

So, I can waste the time I have being angry and over analyzing my pain

Or

Enjoy the time I have

We have to know we can't control time

So, we shouldn't try

Even a broken clock is right 2 times a day

Which lets us know that time keeps moving, regardless of the situation

The hands of time is not what we should fear

We should fear the clock that doesn't have time

That is the clock that gives us no warnings

The one that keeps us on alert, but never knowing why

The clock with no hands is dangerous

So while you are able to see the second hand move...

Enjoy the moment

For at some point, you will no longer have that opportunity

As we look more at time and the forward progress of the world, not only does my story continue, but so do the stories of others. Back in "Tallahassee," I introduced you to a girl who was doing what she felt she had to do in order to try to put things in place to improve her life. Now, years later, we revisit her to see what is going on.

Misunderstood (2/3 of her journey)

She had always been one to let her opinion be known, when she needed to

Maybe that's why people said she needed to learn to be quiet

I've heard those who live in glass houses shouldn't throw stones, so I tried my

best not to

She was both upset and hurt by what people thought, but she never really lashed

out at anyone

At least nowhere near the way they did to her

Well…not until the day came when she could no longer handle the negativity

The respect in which she normally expressed herself was gone

She looked at a room full of people whose only common trait was the fact they

didn't have the highest of opinions of her

"I'm tired of it all.

I'm tired of everyone thinking they know me.

Thinking they know who I am."

Obviously being caught off guard by her words did not change their opinions

"We do know you.

We know you're just a ghetto chick who's just like a walking stereo-type.

Your clothes are too tight, you had two kids before 20 and you can't ever be quiet.

That means you can't seem to keep your legs or your mouth closed."

Debates and disagreements were one thing, but she didn't deserve to be

disrespected

Was she angry?

Of course, but more than that, she was hurt

Crying, she felt it was necessary to continue

"I am not a stupid hood chick."

Giggles came from everywhere

"I may not have a degree like many of you, but that's because I had to drop out of

school when I got pregnant with my first child.

And I know y'all think I'm just a freak who gets around.

The truth of the matter, though, is that my first pregnancy was the result of me

being raped.

Prior to that, I was a virgin who was saving myself for marriage."

The silence was now deafening

"And my clothes, yeah they may be tight, but do you know why?"

Nobody spoke a word

"I do it simply because I'm still seeking attention from males because I never had

that growing up.

So, because of that, I am constantly seeking out a man even though I probably will

never trust one."

Many people, @ that point began or continued to eat their meals

But not the ones they planned

No, they were now trying to finish their crow, humble pie or simply trying to get

their foot out of their mouth

"I am forced to live my life like this

No wait....I take that back.

It's as if the world wants me to live this way.

Is that it? You like the "statistic people," don't you?

I am what I am and there's no denying that.

I accept my flaws because they have made me who I am.

Crazy thing is, regardless of your opinion of me, I'm here.

I'm in the same place, doing the same job you are.

So, do you truly hate me, or do you hate that I've survived?

Do you look down on me because of what you think about me when you should

be disgusted by yourselves because of what you know?"

The spotlight continued to shine on her as she continued her monologue

She smiled

"You know what, I love me! You all have just helped me realize I don't need to

seek attention because it'll seek me.

I now understand all of you! You're like bullies.

You pick on those you think aren't as strong as you.

You attack those who won't fight back.

That was me, but it won't be anymore!

From this point forward, if you want a battle, you'll get one.

I will be respected and nobody will stop me! You can bet on that!"

(to be continued)

Her story is certainly proving how she is misunderstood. Something else that has been misunderstood is my favorite genre of music, hip-hop. I can enjoy the sounds of Nat King Cole or Maynard Ferguson the same way I can Jay-Z , Pusha T or UGK.

The misunderstanding seems to be, at least in part, that the rappers are not the most intellectual of people and those who listen to the music are even worse. I guess part of that belief is because of what gets played on the radio and gets passed for hip-hop. All of the fast-paced music talking about women, cars and money may have it's place, but that's not all the genre has to speak about.

I care about the music, I care about the lyrics.

This is my "requiem," of sorts.

Requiem for Hip-Hop

This is my requiem for hip-hop, calling for a rest from activity for those

who are dead

Not physically, but mentally; those not allowing creative words to live beyond the

confines of their head

Instead, so-called entertainers forget about those who listen to hip-hop for more

than just the beat

Believe it or not, not all fans of rap are just trying to hear about thug tales from

those on the street

Some of us don't care about the economic stimulus plans from thugs

Not all people care about how to get, make and or distribute drugs

And I don't mean to sound irritated, annoyed or irate

But I can't be with the masses because I need my space

Forget a top 8, 'cause there are more than 8 things the people need

And if there are some who are willing to follow, I'm more than willing to lead

If a sacrifice has to be made, I want that sacrifice to be me

And after my death, I hope the music will once and for all be free

My face doesn't need to be on a book for me to receive my glory

My happiness is intertwined with the idea of folks being interested in

hearing my story

I will use notebook pages and concert stages as my pulpit

Preaching my piercing words, acting as if my mouth is a gun loaded with a full clip

I got a itchy "trigger finger" please don't make me pull it

I guess I've been pushed over the edge 'cause I'm tired of the bull ish

So now I'm using that as fertilizer to help my words grow

Seeking to plant the seeds of wisdom while still learning the things I din't know

But I do know that I can't be the only one who cares about the culture

Wanting to get rid of those who feed on dead corporate ideology like a vulture

I am not trying to have a super massive following on twitter where they watch to
see my next move

Life is chess, not checkers, so exactly would that behove

It certainly wouldn't be good for me, so I'll keep them guessin'

Because when someone stays outside of the box, they'll continue stressin'

As I am progressin', I'll smile internally, but show nothing outside

I can't let the world think I suffer from the weakness commonly known as pride

And I also know some say I was set up for failure, especially when I started
actually listening to lyrics

But words need to be heard, so I'll embrace the negativity instead of choosing
to fear it

When I do that, I can make positivity from that negative energy

And since we're all on borrowed time, I thank you for the minutes you are
lending me

Cynically I must show gratitude for your attitude

Because of it, I have no choice but to ascend to higher altitudes

And at first, I admit, I was afraid of heights

So I subconsciously thought my vocal words were wrong, so I began to write

Sometimes me, the pen and paper may disagree

If therapeutic writing sessions are even helping me

But if I never allow my thoughts to break free

We will continue to be shackled to stupidity

You can put the blame solely on me

I'll take that and carry the load effortlessly

The world already has its red pen out, 'cause it's second guessin' while

it's testin' me

I was told this test was multiple choice, so I fail to believe ALL of my answers

are wrong

Perhaps it's you with the incorrect thoughts, so maybe I need to move on

Or perhaps when I ponder, others are supposed to laugh, maybe to them my mind

is the punchline

I may have to withstand the abuse only to prove I'm ahead of my time

So check your watches, do you hear the tickin'

If my objective is to flip words, then I have to sure that my landing I am stickin'

And good riddance to anyone who lacks the ability to listen

I spread the hip-hop whenever I write, I have been chosen for this mission

And I can't even allow other to continue using the nickname Jacob the Great if I

have low self esteem

Just as you can't realistically want fat pockets when your subject matter is lean

So, if you are trying to kill the music I love, get ready to face the charges

Don't say you have heart if what you say shows that you're heartless

Regardless of your trivial words and actions that seem that you want to make the

music stop

The genre will be resurrected

 This is my requiem for hip-hop

One day I had an epiphany. I think I was probably sitting around watching tv or something when it hit me.

I got tired of hearing people asking questions and then some so-called "expert" looked down on them as they answered. Having a degree is great! They show that you have been able to stay focused and learn about something you are passionate about. If you are using that for the betterment of you, your family or the world in general, congrats! However, if you are one of the people who think your degree gives you the right to try to make everyone else feel ignorant, let me just say: "I can't stand people like you!"

I'm not an expert on anything, I've never claimed to be. I just feel there are some things about this world we make far more difficult than they need to be. We all have ideas on how to make improvements, and I think we ignore or dismiss each other far too often. That upsets me.

I've decided to release my opinions on how to solve the world's problems...

I Think I Figured It Out

I think I figured it all out

Yep, every single one of life's questions....answered

See, some people hate the morning because they know the day follows

And simply, they're afraid of what the day may bring

While others hate the night because that brings sleep and we all know sleep is the

cousin of death

Relatively speaking, that is

And speaking of death, what happens when you die

Is there an afterlife?

Do heaven and hell exist?

Well, after your life, people continue to live...

So, yes, there is an "afterlife"

As far as heaven and hell go...if you live your life right, you'll create

heaven on earth

If you don't, please believe your life will be hell

And maybe it's just me, but I'm gonna make sure I'm following God's words and

living my life right first and worry about death when I get there

But what's the purpose of life?

To live it! What else could you possibly think the purpose would be?

You don't have to come up with some "deep thought" filled with big words to

answer that question

It's totally unnecessary and fraudulent

And speaking of frauds, why do poor people destroy themselves trying to act rich, while every time you see a truly rich person, they're acting (or dressed) like they're poor?

Well, poor people sometimes "need" the attention of others, so they do "extra" just to try and show off

Rich people on the other hand just...don't... care!

I mean, they're rich! Why would they care about what us poor folks think?

And I think I know why so many of us do such stupid stuff

Our lives are filled with dumb people using smart phones who don't have enough actual smart people around telling us when we're being stupid

And I have this world hunger thing figured out, too

If we make the countries who eat too much become friends with those who can't get enough to eat...

Boom! Problem solved!

One will figure out how to lose weight while the other will finally be able to gain some

What about racism?

Yep, I figured that out too!

If a person from one race hates a person from another race, it's normally because of ignorance, or because something happened to them in the past they can't forgive and or forget

So, how do you change that?

Well, you simply make two people of different backgrounds actually spend a day together

Allow them to talk and figure out why they feel the way they do

Why they carry hatred in their hearts

Chances are, after a day, their opinion will @ least be slightly altered and that will be a great start

What about all of the other problems in the world?

How would I solve those?

Well, let me provide a single-word, four letter solution...

Love

See, love will destroy hate

Love brings compassion

Love makes you feel wealthy, even when you may not be

Love can make you happy when others may feel you have no right to be

Love is contagious and when you are loved, you tend to spread love

Oh what a wonderful cycle that can be!

But if you've never known love, how can you show love?

I even have an even more simple answer for that...

God

See, I said God because his love and words are more powerful than any problems

we can create

He has laid out the plan for us, all we have to do is follow it

I may not be the most religious person, I admit, but I am learning

Faith has brought be further along than I ever thought possible

So, on this journey, I know I can't make it anywhere without Him

So, yes I may have said I think I figured it all out

But I know God is the reason I feel that way

People like to make things complex. We like to prove we are smarter than the person who wants to simplify things. That's how we are, so it's not surprising. Perhaps one day we will all look back at things others wrote or said and realize we shouldn't have looked at them as being crazy. Maybe they were making a few valid points in the midst of what you thought was ridiculous.

Even when we simplify things, we must also try to be realistic. We have to know the things we want to accomplish can be accomplished, if we put our minds to it. However, we must also know, no matter how hard we work, we will need help somewhere along the road. There is very little we can do on our own.

We have to rely on the networks we built up over the years and call in a favor...

Callin' in a Favor

I try to live right

Try to do what I know is proper

I do this not only because it's right...

But because I want to stay in good terms with both God and karma

I do it because my parents raised me that way

I do it for my spirit

It is done so that not only will people like me, but truly respect me as well

I don't like to burn any bridges

And being any way other than how I am....

Well, it seems like a sure-fire way to quickly burn down every single bridge I

would hope to keep up

But now, I'm in a different place

It seems I need those bridges

But I don't know if they're available for me

Crazy thing is, I had a dream recently

In that dream I was literally trapped by a burning bridge

I was trying to get help, but nobody would listen

I saw people on the other side...

Where I was trying to go and they saw me

They looked into my eyes and saw how desperately I needed their assistance

Yet, they did nothing

I was able to see their faces a bit more clearly after that

I saw they were people from my past

People who I hadn't necessarily done anything wrong to...

But I could also see how they could say I have never done anything right for, either

So, my past actions were halting progress

My past actions were literally about to be my downfall

Why?

Because I had burned those bridges

When I woke up, I felt the urge to apologize

Apologize to all those who I didn't have the greatest of relationships with

Those who I no longer spoke to, not because we grew apart, but because

I was a jerk

I admit, I am not always the greatest of people

I sometimes lack decorum

I am often anti-social

Too often I am told I am brutally honest and that my words, while truthful, hurt

people

And if all that is true, it's no wonder those bridges in my dream were in a

blazing inferno

No wonder that person was looking at me...

Saw I was in trouble...

And did nothing...

I had to change that

Well, I had to start the process of change

And I am still working on that

To those who I have wronged...

I hope they know it was never my intent

To anyone who dismissed me as a person because of something I said;

Please know I understand

I know everyone is not meant to be friends and I'm fine with that...

I just don't like not being liked

I am working on me

God is working on me

So, take another look at me when the finished project is available

I will do the same for you

Who knows?

One day we all may need to call in a favor

Things are not always what they seem to be. No matter who you are, or what you do, there comes a point and time where you will need to look at things from a different perspective. We look at things from our biased viewpoint. I do it sometimes and I know I can't be the only one. Now, in my opinion, it would be crazy to think we will always be able to look at life the way other people do, but sometimes it is necessary.

"Why is that person a thief?" I don't know, but they possibly have their reasons. "Why does that person have low self-esteem?" Perhaps they have gone through things in their life to make them feel that way. "Why does that person hate me just because of my color?" Well, maybe he doesn't.

But, let's just try to look at things from their point of view...

<u>Vantage Point</u>

You became a doctor so you could help

Not just help some, but help everyone

So now, you find yourself temporarily frozen in the e.r.

Seeing blood run away from its owner has become common place, so that's not

the reason you can't move

Then, what is it?

Well, it's the patient's beliefs that have you stunned

The oath you took when become a doctor talked about helping those in need

regardless of race, creed or anything else

But they couldn't have accounted for this situation

See, your patient is a member of the KKK

You only know this because he is still wearing his "uniform"

Maybe he was injured during one of their rallies...

Who knows?

Your mind takes you back to when you were a child

You stayed still with your eyes glued to your grandmother as she told you stories

of her past

How her upbringing was made into a living nightmare because of the 'klan'

How her parents would try to cover her ears and eyes whenever a cross would

burn nearby as they shouted "Nggr, go home!"

"Doctor, what do we do next?"

You are forced out of the past and back into your present situation of saving this man's future

That's when your instincts take over

You forget about how his ancestors probably mistreated yours

All you can remember is how to do your job

And it's a good thing that's all God allowed at that moment because things
would've been different if you would've kept a place for hatred in your heart

Not only would you have not participated in a life-saving surgery, but you would've
never learned who that man was

Yes, he was a member of the klan, but he had certain motives

At one time he was truly lost

He truly believed his race was the only good one

He thought he was superior to all other races, beyond the shadow of a doubt

That is until he met her

Her name was Kristen, and she was black

And that made you wonder even more

It makes you want to know how he could still be involved in such a hate-filled
organization

Well, he does it in hopes of changing others

He figures the best way to help people is to be in the trenches with them

Every meeting he spreads subliminal messages of equality

He has also seen a constant decrease in their popularity and membership

He sugarcoats the 'medicine of truth' in a candy shell so the people who hear him
speak don't even know what has been prescribed to them

He smiles internally as he listens to people who used to use the N-word more than
they had ever said the word love, find alternate ways of expressing themselves

He understood their omission of love was simply caused by hate

But it wasn't hate for others like they had convinced themselves

No, it was simply them not knowing how to ask for help for the discontent they had for who they were

A movement only happens when actual movement takes place

So, your movement will actually help his and who knows...

Maybe those will spark the moments to burn down the bridges to all of the world's backwards thinking

Forcing us to move forward because we will no longer be able to go back

What power!

It's crazy to think we all have the power to force change

Many times, though, we are so blinded by our own thoughts...

By our own negativity...

By our own closed minds...

We can't see the world for what it is, which makes it nearly impossible to envision what it could be

Life, however, should not always be filled with narcissistic views of how we can help 'number 1'

But how we can help others

And many times all it takes is a different perspective

So I ask... are you willing to change your vantage point?

If we take a different viewpoint on things, we may have a different way of thinking... a different way of forming our opinions on people and their lives. I also feel we need to be more honest with ourselves. Many times we try to convince other people we're perfect. We say things like "Nobody is better than me." Well, the truth of the matter is; that statement is a lie.

No matter what it is you do, or how attractive you feel you are, there is always somebody who looks better and can do things better than you. I'm not saying that is a bad thing, though. If we were the best in the world, at anything, most of us would be cool with that accomplishment. We would not work to maintain our level of excellence and we certainly wouldn't work harder to try to improve.

This is not my reality, though. I know this. I am working towards being the best at what I enjoy doing, but I am not there yet. Even if I am recognized as such in the future, I will ignore that and continue to work. I want to be better tomorrow than I was yesterday. That is my ongoing goal. Part of me trying to get better, though is first accepting who I am as a person.

I am not perfect and I won't ever be. My imperfections provide the characteristics that make me who I am.

Flaws...we all have them.

Flaws and All

I've been rejected by girls who said I wasn't tall enough, I guess they thought they were being witty

But yet they later seemed surprised that I said I was too short to overlook their stupidity

It's ironic that folks may make fun of my ears, then they'll talk about me behind my back like I ain't gon' hear

Called me 4 eyes because of my glasses, but with or without optical improvement, my vision of who I am is perfectly clear

I've been told I was too black, but too black for what?

And how can the same person who gets called too black, also get told he ain't black enough?

I ain't ever seen a meter that rates your state of blackness

Or known you can lose some racial membership card because of your actions

Let me retract it, or at least rephrase my statements

For if I feed into the negative, I will fall to the hatred

Never mind, cause that statement will never be true

Giving negativity energy is the same as me trying to lose

And how can one try to lose, if he is fighting to win?

Just as a person can't hope to be forgiven, if he hasn't first admitted he's sinned

I ain't perfect by a long shot, I won't even lie to myself

But I know I have the potential for greatness, I just can't make it without help

So, I take help from those willing to give it, while helping those who are in need

Trying to breakdown stereotypes while building up hope that we all can succeed

In my mind, to know me is to love me, but obviously I can't make that call

I just know if you accept me, you accept me...flaws and all

I'm a flawed individual, sometimes very flawed. Now, I'm not saying that as a flawed person, I can't be awesome. See, in my mind, part of me feeling like I'm awesome comes from the fact that I've overcome some things people consider to be flaws of mine.

Feeling how I currently feel about myself didn't happen overnight. It's been quite a journey (so far). Sometimes, I undoubtedly feel like the coolest person on the face of the earth. Like a rockstar, if you will. Other times, I can't seem to get past the blues. And then again, there are times when I have the bravado of a rapper.

Regardless of what music would represent my mood, I know that God is (Still) the DJ...

God is (Still) the DJ

Remember a few years ago when I told you about that shirt I saw?

You know, the one that said God is the DJ?

I had been thinking about that lately and when I did, it seemed like I was taken

back to that club

Obviously God had become even more popular than before because there was a

line around the corner full of folks trying to get in to see Him work

God is awesome, so it was cool that more people wanted to witness Him!

The crazy sounds He's playing can easily heard outside

It seems like no matter where you are, you can still hear exactly what He wants

you to!

I'm still trying to get in, though

So, I get in line with everybody else

A person with a clipboard can be seen walking around pointing people out and

letting them go in

They are overly anxious and so, none of them get pointed out

I just remain calm

"You, with the fedora, come on!"

I pointed at myself as if I didn't know I was the one she was talking about.

Calmly and confidently I moved into the club

I knew I was gonna hear something from God that would just rejuvenate me...

If I was just patient...

Initially I couldn't even focus on what God was playing, I just watched in amazement as all of the people crowded around Him

They were doing like I was doing the last time

They were trying to make requests, all the while they were probably thinking God

wasn't paying attention to what they were saying

They would learn, though

God is great at what He does

I stood fairly close to the wall for a moment

I watched Him as He somehow used old school records and turntables along with

a digital dj setup

He was mixing all sorts of music, making sure he would be able to reach everyone

And just as the crowd started to die down just a little, he started to play some EDM

I'll admit, that's not something that I listen to, but I know as an entertainer, you

have to reach your entire audience

God was great at that

Soon I found myself moving along with the music I didn't think I liked

I moved in closer, I guess I was trying to speak to God

I knew He wouldn't recognize me, though

I understood He had a lot of people talk to Him on a daily basis and our previous

interaction probably wouldn't have stayed on His mind

At the same time, I really didn't want to bother Him

So, I just nodded my head and "chunked up the deuce"

Like a silent salute

I knew He saw me, but I was surprised at what happened next...

He beckoned for me to move closer to the booth

So I did

"What's up, Jacob?"

When a dj knows who you are, it's a big deal

But when God is the dj and He knows who you are...

That takes it to a different level altogether

"What's up, God?"

I immediately wanted to take back what I had just said

I mean, I didn't want God to feel I disrespected him

Nor did I want to be a southern dude speaking like I was from New York

God smiled

"What's up, son?"

I smiled

I had forgotten God said he had a sense of humor, too

"What are you trying to hear tonight?"

I thought

"I wanna hear something to make me tear the club up."

He shook His head briefly

"You may have asked for something, but did you forget that I do indeed know your heart. And with that, I know that sometimes what you ask for is not really what you need."

I put my head down, almost in shame.

I was a bit embarrassed

"Pick your head up, Jacob. I got you!"

The next thing I knew, God was playing some music that I couldn't recognize, but it sounded very familiar

It was rap, but it sounded like music from the 70s

The hook was a soulful one

I didn't even know I was feeling bad, but the song made me feel better

God had just proven He did know my heart

"That's that new-new!"

I smiled

"Listen to the words and I think you'll understand why the message is for you"

"Yes, sir"

I closed my eyes and listened intently

The song was actually a mix of a lot of different ones

The overall message was about progressing

About "making it"

About loving and showing appreciation for who you're with

About not only accepting where you came from, but embracing it

About prayer

About God and knowing we all have God in us

The mix talked about letting go of fears because we are destined to be great

Slowly, the various songs started to hit me

Flowbots' "Handlebars" faded into Drake's "Successful"

"Empire State of Mind" from Jay-Z and Alicia Keys mixed flawlessly with Rick

Ross and John Legend's "Magnificent"

K'naan talked about being a "Dreamer" while the Clipse said they were "Kinda

Like a Big Deal"

B.o.B. sang "Nothing on You" with Bruno Mars as it was being mixed in with the

smooth instrumental of the 2nd installment of "Maybach Music"

Just for good measures, God then scratched in various rappers saying the name

"Jacob" as Mary Mary let us all know about "The God in Me"

The mix was astonishing

It made me think, though

"God, there's only one gospel song there."

"Sometimes, Jacob, to reach the people you have to have your message

translated so the people will understand it."

And that's why God is the greatest

Nobody in the club was worthy of being around Him

But He allowed it

He came to where we are because He is everywhere

He played what we wanted to hear, but only if what we wanted to hear was what

we needed to hear

He mixed pain with power

He put a fall from glory right next to being on top of the mountaintop

He was letting us all know about life

He was letting us know we can succeed regardless of where we're from

We can be successful if we simply have faith we were destined to

Why?

Well, because the God in us says we can

The God in us says there is no limitations to what we can do because we were

"fearfully and wonderfully made"

At this point I should never be surprised at what happens when God is around

Because He is known for showing up and showing out

So, God, thank you for still rocking the party

Dallas (part II):

After a long time of being away, I finally returned to Dallas. I was a much different person than I was when I left. A lot of learning experiences had occurred and my outlook on things had changed.

I didn't move back to Dallas because I wanted to. It wasn't like I had any animosity towards the city I spent my most formative years in, I just wasn't ready to leave California. Life throws things at you and you just have to adapt to what's going on instead of planning for what you want to happen. During these times, you learn more about your character. Yeah, it's easy to say you would do certain things in certain situations, but when real life happens, you have to put up or shut up and you have to do that very quickly!

After moving back to Dallas, I felt like I was in a foreign land. The places I once knew looked completely different. Some of the people I was friends with were....well, they seemed to be at a different place in their life than I was. When you grow up in a city, around a lot of the same people, you kind of hope things will remain somewhere close to what you're used to.

I had to acclimate to my "new" environment. All of my life I have been the type to be quiet, at least initially. I like to observe my surroundings (even the ones that were once familiar to me). I like to see how the people interact with each other (even if I had previously been introduced to them). My personality seems to make people feel like they have the right to judge me and who I am before they talk to me. Since I have been deal-ing with this all of my life, I can't really say it bothers me. If it did, I would probably talk a lot sooner. Sometimes, though, I question if I should even talk in the first place....

So, for a while, I am quiet...

<u>Quiet</u>

Who am I to speak?

How dare I have the audacity to spread my thoughts

So, for a while.... I have said nothing

I simply observed

I've taken in my surroundings, but have let nothing out

Not my disappointment, not my happiness, not my joy, not my pain......nothing

"Who does he think he is?"

People question my character, but most don't care to hear the answers

Not from me, not from anyone

"I guess he thinks he's better than us."

So lost for words after that statement, I wouldn't know how to respond even if I

wanted to

Anger builds, but my sadness negates it

So, I remain quiet because I have that right

I see so many speak with nothing to say

And I may disagree with what I hear, but I am not now, nor will I ever be in the

position to judge

So I try not to

For I am not better than anyone, just as no one is better than me

As I continue to observe, more and more thoughts cross my mind

Do I speak so I can feel like a part of the crowd, the norm?

And just as I have before, I wonder "Who am I to speak?"

I think about God and the blessings he has bestowed upon me and the
responsibility that brings
Who am I to speak?
No, who am I not to?

Sometimes, we know we should say something, but we don't really know what to say. Sometimes we are forced to be quiet. April 13, 2010 was one of those days for me. In the early hours of the morning, God called my father home. With balloons still floating around in the room from his birthday on April 4th, I saw my father lifeless. My hero's spirit had left his earthly shell. I never wanted to see that day, but there it was.

As the first born son, I found honor in the fact that I was the last one to talk to him alive and the first one to see his spirit had moved on. My heart felt a pain I had never felt, and in the moment, it didn't seem real. The man who I went fishing with, the man who started my love for art and music was gone. The coolest man on the face of the earth....would never again be seen alive.

A little while after he passed, I wrote what turned out to be a song for him, just expressing how I felt. When I was writing it, it felt like he was around. It felt like the words I wrote (and later recorded) were not only inspired by his memory, but also had his approval.

I simply wrote...for my dad...

Letter to Dad

Dear Mr. Gregory Grovey, senior

It's been a little while since the last time that we seen ya

As expected, things are now much different

I've moved back to where you wanted me when you were still living

Yeah, I'm back in Dallas, but it just isn't the same

Not watching your swagger as you call folks "mane"

Dang! Everyday I try to fight off tears

And move past fears just like if you were still here.

It's clear to me I am a long way off from filling your shoes

Praying harder than ever, just trying to get past the blues

I ain't gon' lie, my last trip I swore you'd get better

If folks talked about your demise, I'd be like "whatever"

I was swimming in denial like I was in Egypt

My dad can't die cause I don't understand the reason

But at a lot of times, I can't even begin to understand life

How you gon' leave behind 2 sons and a wife?

It's kinda selfish of me, but I got a little mad

I was pouting like a baby 'cause I just wanted my dad

28 when you died, the same age you were when I was born

Numbers and the circle of life got my heart torn

 Well, everyday that I continue to breathe

I try to be better, 'cause now it just ain't for me

I know it's wrong, but sometimes I fake like I'm strong

Laughing on the outside, but crying when I'm alone

But overall... I think we'll be alright

And I'd do anything for my fam including giving my life

In so many words, you told us to do the best that we can

'Cause more times than not, that's what makes you a man

So now, more than ever I try to live by those words

(And I) try to inspire others even though I'm still hurt

I sometimes feel I carry the weight of the world on my shoulders

And even though I'm grown, some things you don't understand until you

wait and get older

But I just think about the good times whenever I get sad

This is just me sending a letter off to my dad

And I hope God will help me make the delivery

Signing off....love your son... And I mean that sincerely

When adversity hits, you learn a lot about people. Everyone can hang around each other when things are good, but the true test of people and how much they care is how they deal with you when things are at their worst. Now, I most certainly have some good people around me, but during my bad days in Dallas, I found some people just couldn't deal with me when I wasn't happy.

I'm not going to pretend I don't understand, because I do. I was just a little disappointed. See, I'd like to think I'm a good friend to people. Contrary to what I would like to believe about myself, I'm just a regular human being. I, too, have my moments, but when people need me, I'm there. I have been the main person listening in many venting sessions, and I guess I was a little naive for expecting the same when I needed it.

Well, you live and you learn...

Damaged

Banged up, bruised, battered and bloody

Neglected, now negative, feelin' like nobody loves me

My mind's mission is to mend together the broken pieces of my heart

But it seems "hurt" is always headed towards me like my life has a bull's eye and

pain is the dart

Forget forging forward, because life has me facing frauds

Trying to ignore my own ignorance, instead trying to follow the plan that matches

God's

I am damaged

So the things that I want to do, seems to be the things I find that I'm unable

Try to get beyond the shaky ground, but my mind won't stay stable

So, when I move, most of the time I'm falling

In a hurry to procrastinate, why do I keep stalling?

I am damaged

And if I'm damaged, can I even be fixed?

Or do I belong on the island; the one with other misfits?

I'm upset at who I've become

Do I want to face my problems, or do I want to run?

I am damaged and there is no denying

I only fail at life if I give up on trying

So what if I'm damaged, I'm not the first

No matter how bad things are, they can always get worse

"Pull yourself together Jacob", that's what I keep saying

They say life is but a game, how dare you say you want to quit playing

But I'm damaged

So, what! Stop the pity party, nobody's there, but you

You think nobody else has had issues they went through?

Your struggle is yours, but you're not the first to have it by any means

And things may be bad, but not as bad as they seem

So, if you're damaged...cool, that's part of your story

Accept the damage and just move towards your glory

The damaged individual is the one who can help someone else

You're dealing with these issues for others, as well as for yourself

So maybe the things you are dealing with are not things you understand

But maybe your issues can help a little boy become a man

Maybe your problem can help somebody else get better

Maybe your rain will be what provides others with better weather

So, do you still hate being damaged?

No, I didn't think you would

The damage will make you better, your bad will become good

That's if you let it, for that's the reason it's there

You said you're banged up bloody and feel like nobody cares

Well, if you don't care, nobody else will

Your heart is racing with anxiety, so how can peace be still?

You are damaged, but because of that I have envy

Because without being damaged, you wouldn't be in a position for the blessing

God is surely sending

Accept the damage!

To put it lightly, Dallas was not very kind to me. There were many things going on that had me questioning everything. I was wondering why things were happening to me and nothing seemed to be happening for me. I didn't understand why things were happening to my family. Of course I knew nobody's life would be filled with all good moments, but I felt mine was filled with all bad ones.

Then, I started to snap out of it. I realized anyone who has had any breakthroughs in their lives, first had to have problems. How else would they know when they had actually broken through?

When anyone has done, or will soon do something big, they start to notice more people speaking ill of them. There will be more people saying what they can't do than what they can. The biggest supporter of this way of thought is the devil.

I knew it was the devil on my mind causing me to think the way I was about life. I had not been raised to be ready to give up on things so easily, so I shouldn't have been doing it! I got more and more upset with the former angel.

There were a few things I had to say to him...

<u>Dear Lucifer,</u>

Recently I think I've been giving you more credit than you deserve

Sometimes negativity is necessary to appreciate the positive

And I've learned death causes the truest, most genuine appreciation of life

See, I already know you don't care about a person's emotional growth

We all know you would rather see a stunted emotional development instead

You would rather see people in pain, over people progressing

You like it when people actually convince themselves it is not only better for them,

but for the world to play God and determine when their life should end

I know you gleefully watch people such as myself as we get so depressed, we no

longer know who we are when we stare at ourselves in the mirror

Our minds have become so clouded with "your" thoughts, we can no longer even

see God's vision

You have me push away the people who truly love and care about me while I beg

to remain in the lives of those who see me as nothing

It is easier to give up on it all than to actually work on anything

Such is your plan

And I admit, I was buying into it

I was unknowingly a heavy subscriber to your doctrine

But no more

Now I am preparing myself for the fight of my life

The one against you

Now I don't fear you because I understand you

And I would be willing to try to defeat you on my own, but ironically it is now I
realize I don't have to

I have a foundation of family and friends around me (both physically and
spiritually) that allow me to stand tall in the face of adversity

If that weren't enough, I also am trying my best to walk with God

See, I know you hate when people realize they have support

I realize my moments of anger, time of ignorance, temporary lacks of faith, bouts
with depression and sessions of stress have brought you much joy

Just as I am finally realizing it had the opposite affect on God

You won some battles and I can accept my losses, but please be aware that I am
prepared for w.a.r. (winning against resistance)

So wipe the smile off of your face

The demon you were trying to create shall be destroyed

And the Jacob that God, my parents, my brother, family and friends know that I
can be....well, he is certainly on his way

Upon his arrival, please accept your defeat as I have the past and realize your
existence will no longer be relevant

Thanks for listening and I appreciate your understanding,
Jacob

I then started writing to God. I won't lie; because I was still dealing with my issues, I didn't think I would have much to say. However, once I got started, I realized how wrong I was. The words just kept flowing. I guess when you really think about it, that's how it normally goes when you're speaking to, or about God.

What I thought would be a few lines, turned into a few sentences. Those quickly turned into a few pages.

Well, it's a good thing God doesn't limit the amount of time we can spend talking to Him...

<u>Dear God,</u>

God, I know you are a forgiving od

It is only with that in mind I have finally become brave enough to try to speak with you again

Since my last letter, life's transgressions have caused me to...

Well, they have caused me to act in ways I'm not proud of

They have made me behave in ways opposite of how I was raised

In my mind, they have 'forced' me to be something other than who you want me to be

At this point, I wouldn't be speaking the truth if I said I understood my life, so I won't do it

Instead, I will say my current situations are teaching me a lot about myself

They are showing me no matter how far I think I have come, I still have a long way to go

I have now seen things I wish I hadn't

And learned life lessons from those I never thought would teach

I have lost, in the words of my brother, one of my life's life guards

As I wondered why, he simply stated because sometimes God shows us, at some time or another, we will have either have to sink or swim on our own

While I process that, I wade through the water

Hoping... no praying I can actually make it

Foolishly, I sometimes allow my faith to falter

Leaving an opportunity for the devil to invade my mind and weigh heavily on my heart

I would listen as he told me negative things about myself, those around me, and you

It's almost unbelievable the amount of times I believed him

I would begin questions with phrases like, "If God really loved me, then why..."

I would then fill in the remainder of the questions with some random aspect of my life I felt wasn't going right

I think I would keep wondering why things weren't going well

But now I'm realizing, things could always be worse

I once said, sometimes when we feel the weight of extra pressure on our shoulders, we should just look at it as us feeling your hands upon them

Letting us know we may have to be the ones to handle tough situations that others cannot

And while it's true I have never actually asked for said extra pressure, I accept it

Regardless of my sometimes short sighted vision, I eventually am always able to see the bigger picture

And I know that is because of You

As a human, it is in my nature to magnify what's going wrong instead of focusing on what's right

I apologize for that and I pray you don't give up on me

I feel I am simply still under construction and I remain optimistic about you still wanting to see what the completed project will look like

I know you made us all in your image, that's why many of us are scared to look in the mirror

It's as if we're afraid to look at ourselves

Scared to see who we are and unable to look at who you've given us the ability to become

But you know what God? I'm tired of being afraid

I believe I am finally getting to a point where I can see what you have been
wanting me to do for years

I am starting to be able to view the things I want, but don't yet have, not as
failures, but as opportunities to improve

So, I thank you for the opportunities

God, I apologize for taking up so much of your time, but I had a few more things I
needed to say since the last time I wrote to you

With these things now off of my chest, I can now breathe a sigh of relief as I then
try to take a breath of fresh air

How refreshing is this new air?

So much so, that I choke because I'm not used to it

My face is starting to hurt because the smile that's now there is replacing the
frown that had grown far too accustomed to taking up precious real estate

Thank you God for my family and true friends because with their love, combined
with yours, the wall of negativity I had foolishly built up around my heart is slowly
starting to crumble

God, I continue to pray for improvement, not just for me, but for those who have
been placed around me

I have always been told you are the purest, most sincere form of love

And now, I am finally starting to understand that

My life objective is to try my best to repay you, my family and my friends back for
all of the love I have received, especially when I didn't deserve it

Without it, I would have certainly perished, but such was not your plan, and for
that, I am eternally grateful

Sometimes I look back @ my life & I'm given the clarity only you can provide

I look @ some of the more inspirational words I have written and I know I just
wrote them, but they most certainly were delivered to me directly from you

You have given each one of us gifts and I can no longer disrespect you by not taking full advantage of what you have given to me

I'm sorry if I'm rambling, God, but I just was trying to make sure you know the feelings I now have...

The thoughts that have been going through my mind

I know everything we go through is a part of our journey, but I admit, I've had remorse about some of my decisions

About some of the things I have gone through

About myself in general

We are not perfect, I know this, but sometimes I feel we try so hard to be...when we fail, it crushes us

I can no longer allow those type of feelings to crush me

I can no longer let my negativity spread to those I love

In fact... I have to try my best to not even allow the negativity the chance to exist

I know this will only be possible with your help, with your guidance, with your love...

I know this

It has been said we all have to get to a certain place where we will just "Let go and let God..."

I think I have reached that point

It would be unrealistic for me to believe my life will move forward from this point without any bumps in the road

No, but I feel I will now be better prepared for those bumps

God, I guess the point of all of this is to just say thank you

Of course I thank you for the high points in my life, but I would like to thank you more for the low points

To some that may seem crazy, but without them, there's no way we would have any sort of gratification or appreciation when we reach the opposite end of the spectrum

Over the years, my thoughts on life have been wrong, just as they have been wrong about you

I have questioned if you had the ability to help me out of bad situations, when I should have easily been able to see the main reason I end up in bad situations is because I didn't listen to you in the first place

Not only that, but the only way to get out of those bad situations is with your help because when we are left to lead ourselves, we end up lost

God, I am not worthy to speak to you, I know this, but I thank you for taking a moment to hear me

There have been some who have said they won't judge me for my mistakes

Yet they have been very judgmental

There have been some who said they would never leave

Yet, I found myself searching for them, but unable to locate them

All the while, the support that I was looking for was with you

You have constantly provided love and support while accepting me for who I am

You have loved me when I have hated myself

You are the reason I have started to see who Jacob is

You have, and are continuing to show me what life is

I guess it's true what they say...

"God is good all the time...

"And all the time, God is good."

To know God is to at least be aware of the devil, and vice versa. You constantly have a battle going on. You know what is right, you know what is wrong, but sometimes that's not enough. I believe the majority of the people in this world are good. I don't mean good in the sense that everything they do is just what they're "supposed" to. No, by good, I mean people generally don't want to bring harm to others. For the most part, people tend to do negative things because they feel it is necessary for them to survive.

Those who do more good than bad have realized positivity breeds positivity. It may be difficult to think that way, but the things that are most valuable in life are generally not the easiest to obtain. To say I had reached a place of being 100% positive would be a lie, especially when I moved back to Dallas.

Life was happening and most of it was bad, at least that's how it seemed at that point. I fought everyday to think positive thoughts. I tried to pray and speak to others about my issues, but the devil was working overtime on my mind.

There certainly was a battle of good vs. evil, a battle for supremacy...

<u>Battle For Supremacy</u>

The two sides are at opposite ends of the the spectrum

Each has the power to progress, but the other will never let him

Strategic moves counteract those of the nemesis as if it were a game of chess

And although they both grow weary of the battle, neither will allow himself to rest

Because neither wants to confess, @ least when it comes to defeat

They may try to lie to themselves, but couldn't force the other to believe

"You'll never win!" he tells the opposite side

Any doubt is then removed because he's trying to protect "pride"

And that's a slippery slope, one that can easily cause you to fall

It can take you from having everything, to having nothing @ all

The battle has been going on as long as there has been time

The war has been fought for others, and now the battle is mine

My angels fight for me, no matter what the cost

While my demons tell them, "It's over! You have already lost!"

The past transgressions of my life go back as far as the eye can see

But I must realize the war can not be won or lost by them, but only by me

I close my eyes... I see the war zone taking place in my mind and my heart

Heavy artillery is being used, I wished the war was never able to start

But alas, it had, and now I couldn't go back

I just knew, no matter who I wanted to win, I would have to plan my attack

Of course the demons spoke on the negative, they focused on the problems of my

family's lives

But the angels saw the silver lining and talked about how I had survived

The demons said there was no point of trying to live well because good deeds go unseen

The angels said I could live how I was raised, or do the opposite, for there was no "in-between"

But it seems negativity had a point, was this even worth a fight

Did I want to keep my life in the dark, or try to push it towards the light?

The angels felt defeated, so one felt to his knees to pray...

In my mind it seemed over, but then God made a way

"Yes you will have hard times, but so will everyone else...

There is no pain you can ever feel that I haven't already felt"

The voice of God made sense, it provided clarity and understanding

He told me exactly what to do without it sounding demanding

It seems like things were going my way, thanks to what the angels had to say

I guess the battle is over......well.... at least for today

In the battle for supremacy, each side will gain a victory (no matter how slight or grand it may be). WIth me, the evil (or negative side) has, sadly, won way more times than I care to count.

As far as I can recall, when negativity won, it wasn't about me doing something wrong to someone else. Instead, it was about me doubting who I was. It was about me not seeing how much people cared for me. Those were the times I felt I couldn't deal with life and those who knew me would most certainly be better off if I weren't here.

There have been plenty of times when I not only had no fear of death, but I taunted it. I wanted it. I tried to force it to happen. God didn't allow me to have what I wanted during those moments.

But the devil.... he was constantly working on my mind.

<u>Death to Jacob</u>

"So, Jacob how's life? Have you made that million bucks?

Just playing, I know you haven't. Man, your life really sucks!

I'd thought you'd be running things, but you haven't made it far

Didn't you want to end it all? Why didn't you jump in front of that car?

I mean, it was going fast enough, the plan would have worked

Nobody would have missed you, nobody (but you) would have even been hurt

I'm sure the person driving wouldn't have stopped, they would have just kept on

moving

That would have been a win-win, nobody would have been losing

And even if you lived, your life would have been painful, right?

I mean, you probably wouldn't have even made it through the night

You're always ready to quit, so I know you wouldn't have put up a fight

People would have pretended to care, but only until you were dead and out of

sight

See, Jacob you know none of what I'm saying is a lie

So, I'm just wondering, why didn't you commit suicide?"

I didn't really have an answer, but maybe I had more to give

Maybe even though I wanted to die, God still had a reason for me to live

I went to sleep with visions of killing myself, then I would wake up

God please help me stop trying to bring death to Jacob

So, what happens after I wish for, or try to create death? Well, of course I actually have to celebrate life.

When the birthday that forced me to leave my 20s behind finally arrived, I had to think about some things. I had to see where I was in life, compared to where I wanted to be. I had to think about what wisdom would come with entering into a new decade of life.

Did I start to feel old? Not really. See, folks had sort of always told me I had somewhat of an old soul, so reaching that 3-0 milestone just kinda made me feel like I was about to start getting to who I really was.

It's weird, I know, but that's me...

30's the New 20

I heard somebody say 30's the new 20, well that somebody lied

Because the things I wanted to do @ 20 no longer matter because I'm now

preoccupied

Maybe some people say that so they can feel young

But my age just shows how far I have come

For over 30 years I have been blessed to be on this earth

And if time is money, that just means I'm getting closer to my worth

If you know me, then you know I feel like I'm priceless

With age comes wisdom, so now I'm smart enough to know how to handle a crisis

I've got enough life experience to comprehend what life is

And I know anything I may achieve is far less than the promise of potential and

future gifts God just might give

With that said, though, my life hasn't been all peaches & cream

But I've learned you can't wake up from a nightmare if you lose the ability to

dream

It seems as if I've been given a higher level of intellect, so I'll give credit to my age

And if life is full of actors, then it's far past time I took center stage

See, we're all supposed to get our 15 minutes in the spotlight, we all get our time

to shine

I've faded in the background for years, but starting with year 30, I'm taking what

is destined to be mine

Some younger people may say I'm being unrealistic because they may assume

I'm well past my prime

Although I've been praying, hoping and working towards success, I knew it would

come eventually, but only when it was my time

Well, the time clock for failure has reached 0, which means prosperity is up next

And if I can praise God during my low points, His favor will only be the

continuation of being shown I'm blessed

Somebody said 30's the new 20, but I don't care what they say

You see 30 is the same 30, but truthfully, I wouldn't have it any other way

I was thankful. As an African-American male in this country, reaching 30 is almost a surprise. It's sad, but true. Too often we wake up to hear, or read stories about another young person getting killed. That made me think about my people and our culture. It seems we have become too accustomed to death and negativity, but feel awkward with life and positivity. I don't know about you, but that's disheartening to me.

Now, in my mind there's a huge difference between being proud of who you are and discriminating against others.

You don't have to put others down to bring up your people...

<u>W.A.T.E.R. (We Are The Exceptional Race)</u>

We are the exceptional race

Or at least, one of them, we could be

Difficult to accept our fate

'cause faith is what we do need

We try to wash away our past

Of that 'for colored' water

But how are we gonna last

Without raising sons and daughters

In the '60s, it was common for us to get blasted

By those forceful water streams

Trying to get our voices heard and votes casted

Just trying to live the dream of Dr. King

Skip forward to now, do we even care

Our lives are filled with so much potential

But intelligence is looked upon with blank stares

As we battle the capacity of our mental

It's never too late for us to change, though

So let's wash away our negativity for the sake of those sons and daughters

Movement needs to be hasty, no more time for moving slow

And really understand the meaning of w.a.t.e.r.

So now I'm a man over 30 and I'm thinking about many things a little bit differently than I was in my 20s. Almost daily someone on the radio or on tv seems to use the term "real talk." The crazy thing is, the phrase usually was thrown into stories that were full of lies. They would talk about how they had the "heart" to kill a man if the situation ever arose, but they have never even been in a fight. I understand the things they say shouldn't be taken literally because they are entertainers, but sometimes the youth is unable to discern fact from fiction.

A kid will hear a rapper or an entertainer say "real talk," and talk about selling drugs. Then, if that rapper goes to jail, the kid will automatically give them more "street cred" because they feel they are cool for doing what they said in their raps. In reality, that rapper is going to jail for tax evasion and has never been around any drug other than marijuana.

It's cool to entertain, but it's even cooler (in my humble opinion) to be able to take responsibility for what your words may bring.

Hyperbole can be used, but so can reality... That's real talk.

Real Talk

Folks carry around a piece in a backpack, but the concept of peace seems abstract

'Cause they'd rather feast on whoever's on the fast track

their lives spent worried where the crack at and the mack at

And they back at..... the same place where their lives first flashed at

That place where you can't feel safe and folks are quick to find you and try to blast at

Now imagine that, folks still making up lies about slanging drugs and where they trappin' at

And finding fast females trying to mac on that talking bout how they tapping that

You get laughed at while those in control ate pie a la mode and then sat back

You go selling your soul just try to have fun getting funds spitting a verse on a rap track

Silly rab-bit, tricks are for kids, but ain't no kidding around

If you know your stamina's bad, how you think you running your town?

Real gangstas don't play round, so get down and stay down

Real thugs ain't made when you play sounds, you only smile cause they got you playin' a clown

Now face down, cause they got you fooled thinking somebody's rocking to you

You work the streets, give them yo' money, seems like a prostitute

Now hold up, I just tell the truth when in front of a microphone

And if real talk keeps me alone, then it'll just be "I" like with that smart phone

Real talk, my dude, these are my thoughts for food

Humble pie or even crow, man up and accept the truth

What are you doin,' do you even know? Find that if you live fast, then you can't die
slow

Stopping progress, then you gotta go while false talk turns, friends turn to foes

So you got stories about cocaine, and you spit fire like it's lit near propane

Forgive my twang and when I sigh, I think you a lie that's why I be like no "mane"

And if you dope slang, but show no gain, how does that rep for yo' name?

I ain't talking world wide web, but we know you can't run yo' domain

"So lame," that's what the streets actually say the second you turn your back

Don't care nothin' about you and you can just blame yourself for that

They done been lied to and looked down on. You sold false hope in your rap songs

No wonder the love's gone, they get locked up, there's no ET, so no phone home

It's so wrong, but that's the life they live, I think folks like you are to blame

You say you got folks rent around your neck, but wonder why they want yo' chain

Where's yo' brain? They say the mind's a terrible thing to waste, but so is wastin'
time

Time waits for no man, (sarcastically) I thank you for wastin' mine

And theirs too. That don't scare you? We need to find cures like theraflu

But as long as folks livin' make believe, then you don't care who...

So just go wild, i guess i'll just have to be the one to pray for your child

Hope they ain't like you, or end up a victim of lies & end up a cold case file

Real talk, my dude, these are my thoughts for food

Humble pie or even crow, man up and accept the truth

What are you doin,' do you even know? Find that if you live fast, then you can't die
slow

Stopping progress, then you gotta go while false talk turns, friends turn to foes

Please be careful when you say "real talk",

For the lies you sell are the ones that get bought

People act like they still ain't heard,

That there is truly power in words

If you say "real talk", make sure, that's exactly what it is...... real talk

We've all heard that men "ain't supposed to cry." The truth of the matter is that no matter how macho someone thinks they are, there will be a time when tears will fall.

We just have to be careful of devaluing those tears...

If My Tears Had Value

If my tears had value, perhaps I wouldn't give them away so freely

We will all cry. How we deal with the moments that make us feel that way will have a huge impact on us and those around. Whenever we deal with something, the way we feel about it during that time, may not be how we feel when we look back on it. Something good, could actually turn out to be something bad. Of course, something bad could turn out to be one of the greatest things to ever happen to us.

Not everyone has reached their success point yet. Many of us, myself included, are still struggling. Now, we can feel bad about our struggle, or we can realize that it is preparing us to not take our success for granted.

It doesn't matter if a moment is good or bad.. find the beauty in all of it.

Finding Beauty in the Struggle

My struggle is mine, so I take responsibility for it

I admit it exists

And even though "struggle" is usually only seen in a negative light, we must

realize that it too has beauty

We can't appreciate the warmth of the sun without experiencing some level of cold

We can't be thankful for an abundance of rain if we haven't first experienced

some sort of a drought

You can't truly appreciate life, if you haven't witnessed death

See, there is beauty in the struggle

Joy can be found in the pain.... or at least because of it

I have gone through a lot of struggling

But I know you have too

I do not hold the exclusive license on pain

But neither do you

Everyone, no matter how rich or how poor, struggles with something

The rich man may be lonely

The brilliant woman may feel insecure

The jovial kid may be using laughter as a mask...

Covering how he is really feeling

The person who speaks loudly may only be doing so because they struggle with

people paying any attention to them

They struggle with that because for so many years nobody cared

And now they continue to think it is the same way

The writer who writes words of inspiration struggles with confidence

He feels his words are never adequate enough to get across what he is trying to convey

The mother of five gives everything she can so her kids are happy

But she struggles with the concept of love because she wasn't raised around it

Her husband and kids try to teach her what it means to truly love someone

But it is difficult for her to accept it because she's still not used to it

See, the common thread between these and countless other scenarios is that people struggle

They have since the start of time and they will continue until time no longer exists

But just as we have found people who are able to overlook our bad characteristics to see our good ones

We have to find a way to look at struggle and think "Oh, how beautiful this is!"

We should show gratitude for it

We should not run away from the struggle, but attack it head on

Why?

No matter how we feel, struggle happens

Just as death is a part of life, so is struggle

You cannot avoid it, no matter how hard you try

So, if something is unavoidable, why not try to find the beauty in it?

Struggle

Look at the word

Struggle

Say the word in your mind

Say it out for the world to hear...for you to hear

The more you do it, the more power is taken away from it

When something once powerful loses that power, you almost start to feel sorry for it

"Poor struggle. It's so cute how it keeps trying to bring me down, but I won't let it!"

That would be wonderful!

I can tell you.... I haven't quite been able to say struggle is beautiful

But she is starting to look a lot cuter to me

When trying to see the good in whatever life throws at us, we sometimes realize some people seem to be so much stronger than the rest of us. Some people seem to be able to handle things we don't think we could. In my life, beyond the shadow of a doubt, one of those people is my mother.

Over the years I have seen her navigate her way through many difficult situations. When I was younger, I don't think I really gave her the credit she deserved. I guess I thought what she was doing was just what mothers were supposed to do, so I didn't really think it was special. The older I get, the easier it is to see how incorrect I was.

As a man, we think we are strong, but nothing can compare to Mom's strength...

Mom's Strength

Mothers seem to be born with superhuman strength and abilities

At least that's how I feel about mine

I have witnessed things in real life that, in my mind, have turned my mother into a

mythical, magical person

Have you seen a person create a meal when you were sure there were no ingredients?

I have

What about purchasing school clothes when there seemed to be no available money?

Yep! I've seen that, too

When you look at her height, my mother is a small person

But the issues she has been able to carry on her shoulders makes her a giant

She is monumental

She is amazing

Yes, I know I am not the only one who feels this way about his mother, but that

doesn't matter

In the grand scheme of things, mothers are real life superheroes

It's okay for the world to have more than one superhero, because Lord knows we

can never have enough

Mom, let me say I apologize for not always remembering when Mother's Day is

But I would rather celebrate you everyday, not just when the calendar says I'm

supposed to

So, for this day and everyday froward, let me say I celebrate my mother's strength

She handles things I couldn't

She smiles when I would frown

She is positive when I don't know the definition of the word

She is strong

She is wonderful

Thank you Mom, your strength does not go unnoticed

Sometimes we all think we know what's going to happen in certain situations. We may want to rush into action or speak our minds. Sometimes the best way to do anything is to not rush into action, but observe first. When you do that, you usually can get a better understanding of what actually needs to be done. Additionally, you also can see how others are dealing with things that may be similar to your own situation.

As I've said, when we go through things, we sometimes feel we are the only ones in the world to do so. We feel like nobody could possibly understand our pain because nobody has experiences like we do.

For everything you go through, there is someone out there who understands exactly how you feel...

I Understand

The uneasiness you feel when it seems like it's billions against one

Wanting to throw in the towel because you think your life is done

Feeling normal as the dark clouds let loose of the pouring down rain

Uncomfortable in the sunshine because you've grown accustomed to the pain

Trust me, I understand

Constantly feeling rejected because yet another relationship has reached the end

Not comprehending how you pondered the possibility of marriage now she just
wants to be friends

Your calendar of depression only resets after its day count has reached 365

Questions pop in your head like, "Why am I alive?:

I understand

You feel the world has left you, nobody will ever be by your side

Your pain is overwhelming, all you want to do is hide

Whenever you have a moment, the negative controls everything you think

Your problems are sobering, but all you want to do is drink

I understand not just because I am writing these words

But because they are all things I've witnessed, seen or heard

These are only stumbling blocks, look, I've made it through

I am certainly not extraordinary, so you can too

And when you see someone else's life is not going according to their plan

Don't allow them to give up or be depressed, simply show empathy as you tell

them you understand

You know what else I understand and am unafraid to admit? I understand how messed up this country can be! It's amazing some people still don't want us to question anything about this country.

They feel we just pledge our allegiance without question... Well, not me!

The Pledge

We've pledged allegiance to backstab in the United States of hysteria. And since

the public stands for nothing, we're one nation that lacks God, we are dismissible,

without liberty and (with) injustice for all

If you pledge your allegiance to America, you couldn't possibly want to go anywhere else, right? I mean, according to what people say, the United States is the greatest place on the face of the earth. To all the super patriots: don't hate me because I think this country can be better. Don't get upset because I say there are wonderful landscapes outside of the U.S.A.

I don't know if it was the same for you or not, but back when I was in elementary school people would talk bad about Africa and Africans themselves. I always found this strange because the vast majority of the people talking hadn't been outside of the state of Texas. It's all good to love where you're from, but in my opinion it's a bit idiotic to talk bad about, or dismiss a place you've never seen, or people you've never interacted with.

People used to say stupid things like "African booty scratcher." Yeah, I know people laughed when that was said, but I never knew what that even meant and neither did anyone else. Just like it is today, people go along with what others do. That's not cool, at least that's how I feel.

"Why don't you go back to Afica?" ..."Yeah, why don't I?"

<u>Back to Africa</u>

The ignorant, racist white man told me to go back to Africa, the dumb black man said the same

So, from a young age, I've had that idea engraved in my brain

Some will say they need to take all of us and put us back on the boat

That way, they'll get rid of the "blackies," be happy and start to gloat

I guess if we were gone, then they could say their country was once again pure

But they easily forget those native Americans and all of the pain they made them endure

And for the black folks that look down on Africa and the people who live on the continent

Do you understand that is where we all are from? Please, stop making yourself seem so incompetent

In spite of the negativity of what others had to say

I put it in my mind and said I would make to Africa... one day

Sure, it was a dream I wrote down, but didn't know if it would ever come true

Then I asked myself, "If others have done it, why can't the same happen for you?"

So, one day I had a friend from Kenya, who was getting married back in Nairobi

"So, you wanna be in the wedding? What's up Jacob Grovey?"

I laughed at first, thinking it was just a joke

I couldn't go to Africa, I was always too broke

At least that's how I was thinking, but was my thinking wrong?

Well, I always want to try new things, while singing those same symbolic songs?

You know, the ones that say I can't do certain things because they've never
happened before
How I wouldn't have certain opportunities because God would never open those
doors
Then, it hit me, "Why is your glass half empty?
Do you think this an unobtainable opportunity, and it's just here to be tempting?"
Nah, that can't be it, I have to find a way to go
I just have to find a way to hear a "yes," I can't afford to hear a "no"
Next thing I knew, it was April, 2012 and I found myself getting off of the plane
My eyes were immediately opened and my whole viewpoint changed
My heart was beating fast, I couldn't believed I had arrived
Later I thought about how my father was never able to make the trip to Africa and
I had to hold back the tears in my eyes
Nairobi, Kenya was beautiful... much more so than I ever could have imagined
One of my wishes had been granted, but it wasn't because of a genie or Aladdin
No, God, my family and friends made it happen, because of them there was
no stress
So, I crossed one item off of my "bucket list" and wondered what was next
I didn't want to leave and everyone was made aware
If it had been at all possible, I'd probably still be there
But such wasn't my destiny, at least not at the time
The trip did show me if I dream it, then I can make that be a reality of mine
Some Americans may look at going to Africa as a punishment, but to me it brought
nothing but glee
Man, I couldn't believe God let this happen to me
I am forever glad I had the experience and I will always be ready to pack....
For the next time the wonderful continent of Africa says I can come back

When I came back home, I was reminded of some things I already knew. Firstly, there truly is beauty everywhere, if you only look for it. Secondly, God is by far, the best artist ever! What He has created cannot be duplicated. Lastly, I learned how truly fortunate I am.

If you have never gone outside and just looked at nature, you should try it. You don't need all of the calming music and soothing visuals they sell in stores to try to feel better when you're not at your best. Instead, just check out what God has created for us.

And let me let you in on a little secret; looking at God's work is....free!

The Artist

The sun is shining brightly as I just sit and stare

I've been told I'd feel better if I got some fresh air

I'd nod my head as if I actually agreed

But I'd rather watch nonsense on tv than enjoy what God has put here for

me to see

The simpleness of nature's complexities, observing the true beauty of the birds

and the bees

Hearing a conversation as I eavesdrop on the whispers between the wind and the

trees

Do you mean to tell me this art exhibit is being shown everyday?

Created by history's greatest artist and I don't have to pay

My mind draws a blank, I can think of nothing to say

There's greatness in the Lord's design and it is always on display

See, He can see when you're ungrateful for your happiness, so He may add a

touch of blue(s)

He can take your dreary days and add some color to them, too

There's beauty to be seen everywhere, we just have to be careful not to dismiss it

God has put His greatest work on display and He simply calls it "Life's art exhibit"

Austin:

Sometimes you have to make changes in your life in order to make progress. For me, moving to Austin was one of those times. Dallas will always have a special place in my heart and it will always be my hometown. But I reached a point when I realized it was once again time for me to move on.

In a way, I felt guilty because I was once again abandoning Dallas and the family members (and friends) who still lived there. I felt like I was running away from issues instead of fighting them. My second stint in Dallas brought many problems, heartache, depression and pain (with a little bit of joy sprinkled in here and there). I sometimes felt bad for not finding some type of finite solution to all of that before I left.

I soon realized there was no reason for my guilt. Dallas was not a living being who loved me or had done me wrong; it was just a city (albeit the city where I grew up). My friends and family... well, leaving would not change those relationships. Those people who were important to me would not become less important because of their location. So, with this in mind, I started to feel something different.

I felt a strange feeling of hunger...

<u>Hunger</u>

I am hungry

No, scratch that... I'm starving

I'm starving for knowledge

I have a desire to go to the buffet of greatness and overdose on it

My stomach is growling for more

For me to be more

For me to do more

How do I handle the cravings?

I must find exactly what I need and feed on it

How can I desire improvement without knowing the recipe?

How can I cook up resolutions if I am afraid to enter the kitchen?

How can I provide others with the help they need if I'm not willing to serve?

The simple answer is; I can't

So, I must get out of this microwave mentality

Everything I want to do cannot be handled quickly

At least, not if I want things to be cooked up properly

I must understand I have to properly prepare for the meal I want

If I don't, it won't turn out right

And I can't risk that

I know all good chefs started somewhere

So, I can't be afraid that the initial dishes I make don't turn out right

I can't be afraid because improvement only comes after mistakes

So, mentally I start to prepare

I marinate my hopes with sprinkles of my present day progression

I look at it for a moment

As it cooks, I think of how it can be improved

So, I find a way to add my future dreams to the meal

Visions of the finished meal are now in my head

Now, I'm in a hurry, but it isn't finished

I continue to wait

Then.... the timer let's me know time is up

This hunger is about to be demolished

"God thank you for this food I am about to receive. May it nourish me. God, thank

you for taking care of my hunger"

I know I can't be the only one who's been hungry for something in their lives. If I am, I feel sorry for everyone. The hunger can most certainly serve as motivation to do what's necessary to take care of it. When we want something, we try to rush to get it. I do the same thing. When you get an idea in your head, you want to immediately fulfill it.

A sense of urgency is not abnormal, nor is it necessarily bad. However, that same urgency can cause anxiousness and undue stress. It can put the idea in your head that if something doesn't happen in a certain amount of time, then it won't happen. We all do this to ourselves, but why? We are setting these so-called deadlines for our lives, but the truth of the matter is, a lot of times they are pointless. It is wonderful to set goals for yourself, both short-term and long-term. However, we should not get discouraged when things don't go according to what we plan. I constantly deal with this issue.

I know when we plan things, there is a chance things won't go according to those plans. I completely understand this, but it doesn't make it any easier to not look at certain situations as failures if they don't meet the plans. But there is our time and there is God's time. Sometimes they match, and that's wonderful. When they don't, and things don't happen when we think they should, then we are on His time.

And the one thing I learned about His time.... it is ALWAYS better than mine!

Better Late Than Never

I've always heard anything worth having is worth waiting for

So, I can be mad at the fact I haven't reached success, keep hating or..

Know that when it comes to my success, it's better late than never

Perhaps I've only sustained through rain so I can appreciate better weather

Since the moment we are born, we are simply following God's plan

And maybe I wasn't able to do things when I thought, because he knew when I'd

be able to say I can

The journey to get here hasn't been one traveled with ease

But I have to appreciate the bumps in the road because those were the ones

made for me

I think the traps some speak of are simply ones created by their minds

I can't move us forward if I keep checking the rear view to see what's behind

Ultimately, I need to be concerned with what's ahead

And if it's better late than never, then please take heed to what has been said

What do you do when you realize your life isn't going to go the way you thought it would? Do you give up on your goals? There are many goals I (temporarily) gave up on because they didn't happen for me immediately. I later found out there was a reason they didn't happen. So, looking back on it, I feel so much better about how things have turned out.

I'm not gonna lie, though, sometimes when things don't work out, I get in a rut. I get this terrible feeling things will never work out for me. I certainly felt this way when I moved back to Dallas. I lost many material items because of the unexpected move. Additionally, my relationships with friends and family immediately changed. Overall, it was not a good feeling for me.

I could have easily continued to invite myself to my own pity party, but when I moved to Austin, that party no longer existed, no matter how much I wanted it to. Things instantly felt different, even though they really weren't.

I had been given the opportunity to get a fresh start, and I had to take advantage of it...

<u>**Life's Reboot**</u>

Most of us go through our lives doing the same thing every day

We have a routine

We have schedules

We have certain things we have to do, or else we will feel as if our lives our in

disarray

It's like we're programmed

I know normality can be good sometimes, but that's not always the case

See, being programmed to do things make us less human and more machine like

True, this may make us more efficient, but it also makes us boring

It makes us predictable

I understand being predicable and planning has it's place

But so does being spontaneous

Sometimes you just have to throw caution to the wind

You have to sometimes find the courage to go against what you may be used to

and do what you feel you're supposed

Take a leap of faith

Wait! You said you're afraid to anything different? You're afraid to take a leap of

faith?

Well, is everything perfect in your life?

Do you want to improve any aspect of it?

If you want change, how can you get it if you're afraid to adjust?

Albert Einstein said "Insanity: doing the same thing over and over again and expecting different results."

Think about that for a moment

You want things to be different, but you don't want to change anything

How does that even make sense?

I asked myself these questions

Dallas made me rethink many things

It made me consider many different options to how life was for me at that time

It let me know that my repetitive, boring, machine-like life needed to be altered

I needed a reboot

Because of that, God gave me Austin

Never, at any point in my life, would I have believed Austin would be one of my

residential destinations

I was programmed to believe it was not a place for me

I believed it was a very "sleepy" college town

.... With no diversity

.... With nothing to do at night or during the weekend

Well, I was programmed incorrectly

And this is why we must all get away from our preconceived notions

We must sometimes shy away from what others have said about certain people,

places and things

We have to break our programming and reboot

Starting my system over has been a great experience for me

I am seeing things differently now

I am meeting people I never would have before

I am going to places I didn't think I could

All because of a simple reboot

People have always said you can be at your best if you haven't been broken first

I honestly never really knew if I agreed with that...

At least not before now

Now I know better

I have been broken, but somehow I am better than ever

I have been reprogrammed

The crazy thing is, my new programming allows me to not be programmed at all

Now, I'm more of a free-thinker

More open to new experiences

And just improving on a daily basis

I can say restarting my thoughts and rebooting my life has helped me

tremendously

I have to admit.....new Jacob is kinda awesome!

Who knows what it can do for you

......Reboot

I felt extremely blessed about getting the chance to leave Dallas and start anew, but like I said, things initially were really no different in Austin.

The new environment was cool, but every now and again, reality would pop back into my head. I dealt with brief sessions of depression - especially because it took me a little while to find work. I was questioning why things were happening the way they were for me. I just had to take a step back and think.

Think... about what usually happens after the "storm."

April Showers

It's easy to appreciate those beautiful sunny days

That glowing light from heaven just seems to energize us

I mean, how can you be mad when those rays reach you from millions of miles

away?

It's incredibly difficult to do so

On the flip side of things, how are we supposed to fight sadness when we are

going through rain

The droopy clouds make us feel the same

When the cloud lets loose its tears, it's almost as if we are forced to show the

same emotions

We all go through those rainy seasons...

The times when rain seems to pour down on our lives every single day...

Those times when it seems no umbrella can provide any sort of protection...

We all hate those days

It makes us feel like the onslaught will soon force us to drown in our problems

But then, even if for a brief moment, the rain stops

We are given a chance to gather ourselves...

To look around and see if the rain has caused any changes in our environment, the

people around us or in how we feel

We then take another moment to look into the sky

For a little while, we see nothing but the remains off the storm

The skies remain gray

The clouds still seem dangerous

Our environment still feels threatening

Then we start to gain clarity

Those symbolic clouds we had been dealing with start to disappear

We begin to get a little optimistic, but remain extremely cautious

Soon, we get to a point where we want to let our guards down and just try to

enjoy life, but we can't

All we can do is picture those clouds coming back

Now we're getting to a point where our past is disrupting our present

And our present can possibly negatively shape our future

We can feel ourselves starting to get angry as we also begin to lose the little bit of

hope we were getting

Just when we do....

The rainbow appears in the sky

The dreariness of the clouds still remain, but they are being pushed to the

background

The beautiful array of colors soon make you forget about the rain that you just

went through

Before you know it, the sun makes it triumphant return

Now you have a tag team of wonder that is tough to defeat

They make you feel better

They almost make you forget about your problems

It's amazing that just a short while ago you felt lost

You felt as if things would not get better

You saw no way out of the storm

Now, look at you!

You are hopeful

You are optimistic

You are smiling

You are getting back to being who you really are....

And you take a moment to look around

You reevaluate your life

The sun has allowed you to now have a different perspective

You think about the storm again...

Then, for some unknown reason you're forced to look at a nearby field

It's been there all along, but you've never really paid any attention to it before

Now you're seeing all sorts of flowers

The beauty of nature is awe inspiring

You then realize something

As much as we like the sun, we can't survive and grow without the rain

The same rain that we absolutely hate when we actually are dealing with it is
what helps us

It is what helps us be able to handle more harsh conditions as they come along

Thus, it is something we need

The sun, while beautiful, can also cause pain

And the rain, while sometimes annoying, can also bring life

We overlook these things when we are looking at our life

Too much of a good thing can cause you to not really appreciate positive moments

The "rain" will not only make you stronger, but almost force you to appreciate the
"sun"

March is great

So are May and June, but April.....

Yeah, April, in spite of the many treacherous rains I have gone through, is okay
with me

After we go through April's showers, we tend to grow (emotionally). The problems we dealt with and make it through tend to make us stronger. That is a great thing, but it can sometimes be like a double-edged sword. Sometimes being victorious over our problems can instantly make us forget that we were even dealing with any problems in the first place. That is dangerous.

We go beyond gaining confidence in ourselves. We start to get an ego... become over-confident. We start feeling invincible, which may seem okay, but it gives us a false sense of security.

We start to feel as if we are metal, when we are really closer to glass...

Glass

We all like to pretend we're unbreakable

We pretend we have nothing to do with fragility

"Other people can be broken, but not me!"

We tell ourselves lies so often, over time we start to believe they are actually true

We can experience the highest points of life, but if we suddenly crash to the

ground, and have our hearts broken into a million pieces...

We act as if nothing has happened

We act like we're okay

We play "hide-n-seek" with our emotions, but all the while we really aren't trying

to find them

Why?

Well, we'd rather not deal

We'd rather pretend we are a bunch of Supermen and Wonderwomen

But you know what? We aren't! Those are fictional characters

It's amazing to me that we live in an age when we're supposed to "keep it real,"

but we don't seem to have the ability to be real with ourselves

I, for one, no longer want to be like that

I am tired of pretending I haven't been broken...

Because I have

And I don't want to act as if I'm no longer valuable because of it...

Because I am

But at the same time, I will no longer act as if I can no longer pull myself together...

Because that's not true

People want to act like nothing bothers them because they think it makes them strong (or @ least appear to be)

Well, faking ≠ strength, faking...simply = fake

Who wants that to be a description associated with them?

Will anyone raise their hand and say they want to be fake?

... I'm waiting...

Yeah, I didn't think so

Like it or not, there will come a time when you'll be vulnerable

There will be a time when your insecurities will be put on display for the world to see

And when that happens, you have to decide how you will proceed

See, we think once we're broken... that's it

We fail to realize that many things become better and stronger after they have been properly repaired than they were initially

So, if you're like me, you have to quit denying your past

Quit denying your pain...

Acknowledge it all because that's the only way we can move forward

I know sometimes being the first to admit to pain can be both awkward and intimidating

So, let me take that load off of the mind of everyone who is afraid to do so

Hello, my name is Jacob

I have been broken several times in my life

I had assured myself that I was not worth the "repair"

I told myself I was getting what I deserved and that it wouldn't ever get better

But I was wrong!

Through the support of those around me, I rediscovered the power of prayer...

The power of faith...

The power of God...

And because of that, I learned about the power I had been given

That's when I learned that people can and will always try to break us beyond what they think is repairable

We can only actually get to that unrepairable point when we allow ourselves to go there, though

I've decided to lose the ability to put myself there any more

Don't get me wrong...

I may crack...

I may break...

But I have faith that God will put me back together

He will repair me as He sees fit

So, I welcome all of life's challenges

I welcome all of my challengers

I welcome my haters and those who try to detract my while hoping to detach any view of optimism

Yes, we can be compared to glass because we are fragile, but we also have to realize how tough glass can be

Glass can harm those who try to break it

Of course, I'm not saying we should try to harm those who desire to break us

We should just make sure they have a reminder of who we are

Who we are trying to be

And how tough our spirit is

Leave them with them with these simple words...

You will not win because I will not lose!

When I think about how fragile we truly are, it makes me want to escape reality for a little while. So, what's the easiest way to do this? Well, I know what some of you may be thinking, but it's not drugs. The answer is television.

It's kinda weird that we look to escape our reality by watching "reality" shows. We are too busy in the real world to ever take a break and sit down, yet we easily waste time with sitcoms. We say we want to see more positive things on the screen, but we support the most "ratchet" things we can find. I know this first hand. If you take a look at my DVR, you will see a lot of these type of shows on there. I'm guilty, I'll admit, but at least I know I have a problem.

What we watch can greatly bother what we are doing in our actual lives.

Somehow, I need to find a way to get back to life...the program at hand.

Regularly Scheduled Program

Television is supposed to be a temporary escape from the way we really live

I've seen too many men not care about their significant others, but are always watching the basketball wives

Women will complain frequently about their guys wanting to chill out on Sunday to watch the NFL

But they'll watch TMZ to see which players are married, cheating or who have recently gone to jail

A family won't have dinner together because excuses are made and they'll say they're not able

But then you'll find various members sitting down to watch the Huxtables at their dinner table

We can sit down with our kids to see "Beyond Scared Straight"

But when a kid is having real life issues with peer pressure, the parents will tell them to wait

The next thing you know, the kid gets locked up and the parents don't know why

They'll say they don't know what went wrong with their baby because all they know is that they tried

But that's a lie, and the truth shall set them free

They won't admit they weren't watching their child because they'd rather watch tv

We can watch all of episodes of CSI to try to figure out the crime

But we fail to realize our neglect is killing our kids, it should be us doing time

If you won't admit to being part of the problem, let me go ahead and say I am

Now, you can get back to watching reality or back to your regularly scheduled
program

In the case of the young lady I told you about (in both Tallahassee and in Riverside) her "show" didn't always go the way she thought it would.

The program that is scheduled isn't always the one we end up seeing...

Miss Understood (3/3 of her journey)

Back in '09, she was misunderstood

She took abuse because of what people thought about her

She convinced herself she was beneath others...

That she was worthless...

That her life had no meaning...

One day she had an epiphany, though

She realized the opinion others had of her meant nothing if she didn't go along

with them

So, as it difficult as she was, she stopped agreeing with what they thought

She took a long hard look at herself

When she did, she saw herself in a different light

Sure, she was able to see her imperfections

But she was also see her inner beauty

She was able to see why she was unique

Why she was worthy of love

Why she was not supposed to just take the verbal abuse from everyone she met

She came to the conclusion that everyone has a past

Yes, she had gone through some things she wish she hadn't

But she couldn't change what had already happened

She had to stop feeling like she had to play the role of the victim for the

rest of her life

Her past life tests were now just a part of her testimony

Nobody could take that from her

At one point she said she wished her life would have been different

But she no longer feels that way

She accepts every aspect of her life

It all brings her pride

She feels blessed to have her job because "on paper," she knows she isn't

technically qualified for it

She is proud to have kids, even though their conception wasn't planned

They now serve as her motivation to continue to persevere

Her past experiences are now stories to tell young ladies when she speaks at

various high schools across her city

The young ladies who hear her speak know she is telling the truth,

so they respect her

She lets them know about her mistakes, her survival and her inability to give up

They see she only wants the best for them

Some of them don't have that in their lives

And if they didn't hear positive words from somebody they had respect for, they

may end up falling into some of the same traps she did

Thus, the cycle would continue

She couldn't allow that to happen

Her outlook on life was now more positive than the majority of the people she

worked with

Most of her peers were miserable, even though it seemed they should have been

happy

And seeing how they used to treat her, she could have found happiness in that

But she didn't

There was no need for her to have ill feelings towards anyone, even if they still had them for her

She was in a different place

She wanted everyone to be close to where she was

Not to where she used to be

She recalled her life and she was amazed

She was once stripped to her soul

She fought and fought, even though she was misunderstood

Now, we are seeing how she has made it through all of that to be independent

To be strong

To be thoughtful

To be caring

To be at a point where everyone "gets" who she is

In other words...

...To be "Miss Understood"

As a man, it is easy for me to admit I don't always understand the logic of how women think, but I can't deny how amazing they are (even when I'm upset with one of them).

Women are special, and I don't think we tell them this enough...

<u>Woman</u>

No matter the struggle, the pain, the desperation or the plight

Life never seems to have the ability to take a way a woman's willingness to fight

She soars above many when some don't want her to take flight

Try to take away her sunshine, leave her life permanently dark, as if it were the night

They have a certain glow about them, especially when they smile

Most are nurturing and attentive, as if taking care of a child

What some consider nagging, she calls showing concern

She pushes for the greatness of others, as she patiently waits her turn

I am amazed at their tenacity, so I sit back and observe

She's strong enough to handle our fears, although we couldn't handle hers

She is inspirational, and her influence knows no bounds

Our world is infinitely better, strictly because she is around

She works hard every day, this is why she survives

Everyday her spirit is better, so to be like her... we strive

She is power, she is beauty, she is honor, in a world of lies... she is the truth

Yes, there is a God and the fact the He created women is the proof

As you can tell by the last piece of work, I have no problem showing admiration to those I feel deserve it. Sometimes it may take me a while to give a person credit for the positive things they have done, but eventually I'll get to it. One person I wish I would have said more to about how much I admired them was my father.

Over the years, I'm sure I had to tell him a few times and I'm sure he had to know, but I could have verbalized it more. As humans, every so often we need to hear others say things we already know. I guess it's for validation purposes. Now, my father is gone and it is too late for me to tell him face to face, but it's not too late for me to tell you about him. So, that's what I'm going to do.

<u>**Lessons Learned**</u>

Education in this country is very expensive

But how do you repay a person whose teaching was relentless?

Giving you lessons every day of your life

Teaching you how to be a man, care for your family and treat your wife

And what makes it even greater is that he was a volunteer

While some folks would leave, my father was right here

Some would show no emotions, but my father showed he cared

Sometimes he would help me along, while other times I would be left alone just to
see how I fared

I didn't always understand the tactics when I was young, but now it makes sense

I understand that we sometimes must open up to express ourselves for happiness,
just as we may need to vent

To say he was cool would be an understatement and anyone who knew him
already knows

Any cool aspects of my personality are passed down from him,
and I'm sure that shows

Knowing Greg Grovey, Sr. was an honor, it was a right I would have
gladly tried to earn

But God blessed me with his presence for free and I thank him for the lessons
learned

Not only have I learned lessons from my father and mother, but also from my younger brother.

To me, he is a very intelligent young man with the potential to do something incredibly important in this world. In many ways he has taught me how to look at the world differently. The way he sees and reacts to things is very different than how I do. We tend to take our siblings for granted

Little brother, I just have to let you know, that's not the case...

Little Brother

1 day before my 5th birthday, you were born

I remember trying to climb the wall so I can see you in the nursery window

I didn't understand why everyone didn't want to pay attention to me

I mean, I'm Jacob

I was the young member of the family that everyone always wanted around

That day, I was an after thought

I won't lie and say I wasn't jealous

Because I was

I was also upset

Who were you to come and steal my thunder?

Just because I was selfish and stupid, I didn't like you

And when you came home, I saw everyone still trying to be around you...

So I tried as well

I tried to pick you up and push the stroller and everything I could do to find a way

to get attention

But as I did that, I found myself actually finding out what the fuss was about

You couldn't speak, but your personality was different

You were not just something everybody thought was cute

You were an actual person

As the years passed, I saw how smart you were and at some point I became the

proud older brother

I didn't want any harm to come your way, so I did everything I could to keep you protected

I had my friends look out for you, just as they looked out for me

Any teachers that knew me had to learn who you were

Now, you're grown

And saying I'm proud of you is an understatement

You have a much higher level of focus then I do

I admire that

Your work ethic is like Mom and Dad's

I'm striving towards that

And your spirituality and relationship with God is inspiring

I'm working on that

My actions may or may not show how happy I am for you and

your accomplishments

But hopefully these words do

I couldn't have asked for a better brother

I have to admit something. Not only do I sometimes miss out on opportunities to speak positively about my family, but on far too many occasions, I miss the opportunity to speak about God. Sometimes I feel my lack of knowledge about God is embarrassing, so the devil makes me feel like I shouldn't speak. Sadly, I go along with that.

I know for a fact none of us are truly worth of speaking to him, but in spite of that, he allows us the opportunity to do so anyway. Even with that, I feel like I am not ready to speak. Maybe it's because I know I'm still a work in progress.

Maybe because I know when God wants me to speak, I will...

<u>(untitled)</u>

God, when I am silent, I know you hear my thoughts

At times I lack the intelligence to vocalize what I am trying to say to you

But I know you can feel my heart

My spirit sometimes get heavy

But when nobody else can lift me up, I know you can

When the sun leaves the sky, covered by the clouds, it is as if you are shielding us

Shielding us from your light because we can't always take it

Instead, you may choose to give us rain

The rain washes away our past and is the foundation for the growth of our future

I thank you

And the devil is always at work

He employs millions to do as he does

To think as he does

But, even in the midst of a recession

Your word lets us know you are forever hiring

Lord, I simply ask that I may turn in my life application to you

You may not give me the job now, simply because I may not be ready

But I ask you to work on me

Train me in the ways I should live so that one day I may be "hired"

Seasonal, part time or full time, when you say I am ready.. I am more

than willing to work

Lord, sometimes I am silent

But when you say the job is for me to speak on your behalf

I'll be ready

One of God's greatest creations is women. With that being said, though, there are some issues and problems I believe women bring upon themselves. Sometimes simple things quickly turn into complex things because they make them that way. Now, I'm not saying us guys don't do the same thing every now and again, but it seems to be the "norm" for women.

Perspective with anything is very important. This does not exclude the male and female dynamic. Women, the issue we sometimes have is that you won't admit you have imperfections. Yes, we like you the way you are, but you have to know that we ALL have issues.

One issue some women have is they are too...materialistic.

But do you know why you're looking for the materials you have in your sights?

<u>Material(istic)</u>

Women, you often say you are looking for boyfriend or husband material

The problem is, you seem to be "shopping" for that material in the wrong places

I understand everyone likes to find a deal, but you really shouldn't expect to find

the high-quality, rare material at your local thrift-store

If you're looking for material that will make up your companion

You may not find it in your local club

If you're looking for people cut from the cloth of faithfulness

You probably won't find that in the bar

When searching for the material that shows a spirituality

You probably won't find that in places where God is taboo

Women, you should not settle for any materials

Just because you find they are plentiful

Just because they may look good to you

You have to search for what goes well with you

What you are looking for

The type of material that would stop you in your tracks and make you stop

shopping altogether

Women, sometimes it's okay to be materialistic

As long as you're looking for the right material

Yeah, there are certain things women look for (or should) when it comes to their companion. There also are certain things us guys look for in a woman. Outside of all of that, there should be things we look for when we look at ourselves.

What is it we are hoping to accomplish? How do we actually reach our goals?

Are we even able to take care of the things in life we hope to have?

<u>Jacob's Ladder</u>

Ascension is my intention, but I'm afraid to reach new heights

It seems my success has been stunted and I can't get my life right

Am I prepared for prosperity, or more prepared to be poor?

Am I ready to shop for success, or scared to know what's in store?

Wait! My name is Jacob, so it's normally associated with a ladder

So do we subconsciously try to live up to our names, or do our names not matter?

I believe my name is mine because it is wrapped up in my fate

Jacob is a biblical name and his outcome was great

But he had to wrestle with many issues and I have had many as well

The issue is not with falling down, but trying to get up after I fell

I know sometimes I have had issues regaining my footing, it seems I am not on stable ground

It seems I can't always reach out for helping hands because it sometimes seems nobody is around

But honestly, I know that's not true, it's just the devil playing tricks

Whenever I'm doing well, he wants to convince me I'm still incredibly sick

But that will no longer work because now I'm ready to climb

I will ascend my own symbolic ladder so I can claim what's mine

So, the people that have previously tried to pull me back, will now see me press on

I am trying to leave my self-doubt in the rear view and make sure those days are gone

I think I've always had the keys to success buried inside

It's like I knew my destination, but I was too afraid of the drive

But I've gotten a little older, a little bolder in my actions

I don't care if the ground is still shaky, I'm able to gain some traction

I know people will continue to talk bad about me, but neither that, or the doubt I

sometimes have no longer matter

I can no longer be afraid of my ascension, I must prepare to climb Jacob's ladder

In addition to improving myself, it is a goal of mine to improve the world. Lofty goal, I know, but in order for me to do that, I have to first improve our communities.

It has always saddened me that in "urban" neighborhoods, you would usually find a liquor store very near to a church. Sinning and salvation go hand in hand, but that's a bit ridiculous.

It's as if the neighborhood planners intentionally put them together to force the minorities to choose...

Churches & Liquor Stores

The preacher tries to rejuvenate spirits, while the liquor store has spirits for sale

The church wants to learn about our Savior sitting in pews, while the store will

have people spewing about their alcoholic tales

The liquor store is full of people trying to get the drinks that'll make their party pop

The church tells us not to (judge and) throw rocks while liquor stores have setups

for Ciroc

So, let me ask you this; what exactly is your favorite flavor?

Do you want some coconut rum, or taste the salvation of our Savior?

Are you willing to give up some of those drinks to get God's favor?

Or you want to party now and worry about repenting much, much later?

I am not one to preach because I am certainly in no position

But the church, or the liquor store? That's one tough decision

Do I want God or a drink?

Clouded judgement or freedom to think?

Do I want to not deal with my issues and party, or do I want more

Well, we have the choice...church or the liquor store

I have never had to deal with the pressures of alcohol getting to me, but I have witnessed the problem it has presented to others firsthand. On the flip side of things, the purpose of the churches that normally sit very near those liquor stores is to help us learn to deal with life and to grow in our relationships with God. Sometimes we are too weak to even realize that. Sometimes we don't know how we're supposed to feel about anything. Sometimes we feel like we own the rights to problems because there is no possible way anyone else is going through the same thing. Just when you truly try to convince yourself of that, you turn on the radio and you hear something that reminds you of your story.

Music has a way of making you reflect. You don't have to be listening to a so-called "thought provoking" song to actually making you think. You don't have to be listening to a "ratchet" song to make you feel like you want to tear something up. A gospel song is not required to make you feel something in your spirit. The point of it all is that music is a means to make you feel something.

Music lets you know you are not alone in this world...

Music Makes Me Feel...

Music makes me feel like I have the ability to be immortal

Be socially awkward, yet still force everyone to always remain cordial

Have two turn tables and a computer work side by side with a band

Make the arrogant new school respect the genius of the classics as they all work

hand in hand

I feel the political energy of James Brown, so I can mix it with that of 'Pac

Both having different, yet similar views of how to make the social

discrepancies stop

In my head, I hear smooth Nat King Cole vocals combined with futuristic tracks

by Timbaland

Making the hipsters, thugs and the older generation all get together and dance

Music makes me happy, it makes all of my problems vanish into thin air

And those minor things that were stressing me out, well, about them I no

longer seem to care

Jill Scott makes me want to take "A Long Walk" whenever I need to ease my mind

While Miles Davis tells us even when feeling "Kind of Blue" we're still one of

a kind

And at the same time, Earth, Wind & Fire help me feel the spirit of my dad

As I hear the words "Keep Your Head to the Sky," just as he had

Music can help you find memories you never knew you lost

The music on a cd, mp3, album or tape can feel like the best thing you

ever bought

Sometimes you can't believe your own emotions because they feel so fake you think they can't be real

When I can't express myself, the music can say it all for me, at least that's how my music makes me feel

Music makes me feel a certain way, but so does love. I haven't really been many places in this world, but I was starting to feel like somewhere along the way, I lost love.

I wanted desperately to find it again...

Lost and Found

Like misplaced luggage on a flight, I had lost the idea of love and never thought I
would get it back
My memories were like the carousel at baggage claim...
They kept going around and around, but I was never able to get what I was
looking for
At first I was okay, but as time passed, I kept seeing more and more claim what
was their's
I didn't have that luxury and it began to get to me
Why was bad luck the only luck I had?
That was the million dollar question and I had no idea how to answer
I waited and I thought
I sometimes stood in anger, other times I was pacing in confusion
I wasn't read to give up only because I already had
I made a decision to try to convince myself that the baggage that came along with
love may have been too much for me to handle
Maybe I would be better off without it
I mean, we don't all actually need love, do we?
I had always considered myself to be a bit of a loner, so I should've had no
problem being alone
The problem was, I wasn't just alone.....I was lonely
I know you aren't supposed to, but I envied others
I wanted what they had...

What I couldn't seem to keep....

I wanted to love and to be loved

In theory, it was simple, but theories often become more complex when we try to put them in practice

"They" always say practice makes perfect, but that's a bit misleading

Like I heard from one of my teachers growing up, a better way to say it is, "Perfect practice makes perfect."

See, if you practice incorrectly, your outcome will match

That's the problem with love

Each time we enter a new relationship, it means we failed in some aspect of the last one

In essence, we practiced incorrectly

To actually improve our relationship, we can't "practice" the same

We have to learn and move on

That's easier said than done

This is why the symbolic luggage remained lost

For a while, I just couldn't accept the fact some things were missing and no matter what I did, I wouldn't be able to get them back

That can certainly be a tough pill to swallow

But as difficult as that pill can be, it is necessary

It is needed to get better....to move past what made me ill

So, what was I to do?

I knew what I was "supposed" to do or what I could do, but not really what I should do

After waiting a while, I told myself something needed to change

Perhaps I had to look outside of the places that would normally be searched

This luggage was special

So, I closed my eyes for a moment

Blindly I let my heart lead for a moment

I didn't know where I would end up, but I had to step out on faith

When you step out on faith, that means you're no longer leading yourself

Instead, you are humbling yourself and following God

When that happened, I received a message that was delivered directly to my heart

It said what I was looking for had been found

I would no longer have to search

I had been told that before, so I didn't want to get my hopes up too high

But then I met her

I soon realized the high hopes I was fearful of having were actually very far

beneath her

She was the personification of amazing

Her smile lit up the night sky

Her eyes had a sparkle that easily could have found a home among the stars

Her skin was only subtly touched by makeup which allowed her God given beauty

a chance to shine

Her body was what dreams were made of and seeing her in front of me was

almost unreal

She spoke as if she was unaware of her elegance

So grounded, so personable, so wonderful

She was like the next level of what I wished for, but more than I thought was

obtainable

And God sent her to me.....wow!

All of my past tribulations were forgotten, instead I remembered what "hope" was

She was refreshing, quenching the thirst of what I desired

Replenishing the energy I had lost

She was astonishing without trying

She was just being herself, which made her more incredible

Looking back, I admit I lost the idea of how love was supposed to feel

I lost hope in it

It seemed more farfetched the older I got

But she let me feel the way I once had

She helped me locate happiness

I closed my eyes again, but this time my head was pointed towards God

I silently thanked Him over and over

I opened my eyes only to see her looking @ me

The carousel of love's memories passed in my again briefly as I looked @ her

This time there was something that seemed familiar

It was like something I knew, but a better version of it

I saw it had my name, so I reached for it

When I fully snapped back into reality, I found myself reaching not for a bag, but

for her hand

My mind would only allow me to say one thing

"Hello love. I'm glad I was finally able to find you again."

Without love, we all would truly be lost. I may think about love a little too much. It weighs heavily on my spirit and I admit that.

My viewpoint on the world may be more optimistic than others at times and more pessimistic than others during the other times. Part of the time, when I feel a sense of pessimism is when I think about death.

But before death, I think about extinction...

<u>**Nearly Extinct**</u>

They are a strange group

At least that's how many view them

Most of them are being held in captivity

Many times they are viewed as ignorant and angry creatures

It doesn't take much to understand that if you put a species in hostile

environments, it's only a matter of time before they become hostile themselves

Does that excuse them?

No, but it should help others understand

It's sad when you look at them

They pretend to be one thing, but their eyes sometimes show they are sad and

afraid

Those in control have scared them so much that they've become overly defensive

In turn, those in control now fear them

They abuse them to try to show they are still in control

The abuse helps the anger build

Now they don't trust the "hand that feeds them"

And rightfully so

The hand that feeds them is also the hand that beats them

So why shouldn't they be ready to bite that hand

They are called ungrateful

I guess they should appreciate the mistreatment

But for some strange reason...

They don't

So, now they are in a dilemma

They know in order to quit being abused, they actually have to work with the one responsible

But how are they supposed to do that?

How can they even believe that is an option?

How are they supposed to trust those who terrorize them?

How are they supposed to speak on the treatment if they are constantly being muzzled?

How are they supposed to get better if they are only around what made them sick in the first place

They are black men in America

And I am one of them

We are nearly extinct

And those in control wouldn't have it any other way

So, it is our responsibility to break out of the dog house to get houses of our own

We have to quit depending on them to feed us so that we can help others feed themselves

We have to stop giving them any kind of reason to say we fit the description...

The description needs to stop matching us...

We need to believe we can be positive

Which will force them to stop believing we are all negative

In spite what we sometimes want to believe...

We all need each other

We need them

They need us

We are nearly extinct because we choose to be

We choose to help them kill us

We choose to accept injustice against us

We are silent when we need to make noise

And noisy when we have nothing to say

We are nearly extinct

But believe it or not, we don't have to be

So, black men, I ask you the following...

Will we remain endangered?

Will we make the smart moves to preserve our species?

Or, at some point will we end up being called dodos because we had the same

fate?

Or... will we shock the world, realize our brilliance and start working together

instead of against each other?

Only time will tell, but I'll tell you this

I value the lives of others way too much to just allow the same to continue

I may not be the one who will be recognized for changing the world

But I just want to be able to say I was a part of the change

Ghandi said "Be the change you want to see in the world."

Such is one of my many goals

And yes, many will say we are nearly extinct....

But you know what?

We ain't gone yet!!

To me, it not only seems like the black male is extinct, but also the confidence of the black woman. I know some people will read that and immediately disagree, and that's fine, but I want you to think about something for a moment. How often do we see a black woman who is so confident in herself that she doesn't feel the urge to hide who she is? How rare is it to find an African-American woman who doesn't have a combination of fake nails, hair or even fake eyelashes? I'm not saying anything is wrong with that, trust me, I'm not, but how confident are those ladies in who they are?

The confidence things isn't all about the cosmetic, or "look" of the woman. Women are brilliant, but too many times they feel the urge to dumb down their intelligence because of their friends or even because of men. Women, be proud of who you are! Be proud of what you know and what you've accomplished! Women, you don't have to be "fake" to be loved.

I am a fan of those who are naturally natural...

Naturally Natural

Shout out to all of the women who ain't worried about havin' that "Hawaiian Silky"

hair Just 'cause that's what so many others have

Just know, I am not disrespecting those who are unbe"weave"able

Go ahead and do your thing

Just know that these particular words are not for you

Nah, this is for those with 'fros

Those who exist with twists

Those girls with curls

The ladies with locks

And even those who can't leave home with out their straightening comb

This is for those who just let their "soooooooul glooooo"

Now, they may use a little bit more than juices and berries, but their hair is still

natural

And don't think it's just about those with natural hair

No, no, no

This is also for the women who wake up

And don't have to cake up the make up

I mean all of those who have that natural shine

That God-given glow that stems from their spirit to their skin

The beauty on the outside is enhanced because of what's within

I'm talking about the women who's main source of blush can't be bought from the

store

No, their blush comes from the blood rush when she hears a compliment

I'm talking about the girls who ain't afraid to strut and show their confident

She's naturally natural

And naturally the natural girl will come in different shapes

It doesn't matter if she's a size 2, a 4 or an 18....because she's still a 10

When you get close, she smells like vanilla

Enchanting and flavorful

Ain't no plastic surgery with her

She's all real

She's keeping whatever God gave her

She ain't worried about having Barbie's appeal

Man! That natural woman....

Again, all women shine bright and I ain't thrownin' no shade

I just had to shout out to all of the women who are naturally made

Destination Unknown:

"We don't know exactly what's going to happen in our futures. We do, however, know what we want to happen. We have more control over our hopes and dreams than we tend to believe, but we sometimes are just afraid of that much responsibility. What do you want out of life? Better question, how how much are you willing to sacrifice to get it?"
— Jacob (2013)

Very often, you will hear a man say he is looking for his queen. We say we are search-ing for the woman that deserves to be treated well. Contrary to how popular that sort of thinking may be, I feel all women need to be treated well. Perhaps the most angry, bitter and upset women act that way because they may be in desperate need of said treatment - simply because they have never had that before.

But how can we, as men, be searching for queens if we don't know we are kings? Our treatment of others stems from how others have treated us. For some of us, many questions can easily be raised. How can we expect to protect when we have never felt safe? How are we supposed to know how to provide for our woman when we don't feel we've ever been provided for? Doing things that have never been done before are difficult. It benefits us all to pass along wisdom we learn along the way, especially about how to treat others.

If we are truly looking for queens to be by our sides, first, claim the crowns that rightfully belong to us...

King Uncrowned

We were born with a sense of entitlement

As a baby, one of the first things we learn is; when you cry, others are supposed to

come running

You are special and you know it

As we get older, for some reason, many of us stop feeling like we're special

Maybe those who are older than us stop treating us like the unique gifts they once

did Because those older than them did the same

It's a vicious cycle we sometimes are unable to break

So, let me try to break that cycle right now

Let it be known, the following is not to be seen as any sort of super bravado

It's not so that I can try to belittle anyone

It's so that I become familiar with who I am

So I can find my place in the world

See.... I am a king

I was made in the image of God

So, contrary to what anyone wants to try to convince me of...

I am special

There is nobody like me

I don't care if we were born on the same day

We are not the same

I don't care if we look alike

We are not the same

We can walk alike and talk alike

But being alike doesn't make us the same

If we share similar personality traits, you know what?

We still aren't the same

You are not like me

I am not like you

I am a king, but I have yet to be crowned

Let it be known...

You, too are a king

However, it would not be beneficial for either of us if I try to help you find your

throne

For I have not yet found my own

I am not yet in a position to lead

But I am working on it

I KNOW I am regal

My heritage tells me, in spite of all that went wrong, my lineage is a glorious one

In spite of my present day troubles, I KNOW my future is a bright one

For I have faith that what God has told me shall come to pass

I KNOW what He has destined for me is far greater than any of the struggles I

have, or ever will endure

They say "heavy is the head that wears the crown"

So are his burdens

So, God is preparing me for those burdens

He is preparing me for my crown

He is getting me ready for my glory

And although I may sometimes think I know what's best for me

I'm sure God always does

So I will trust His knowledge

So, should I feel entitled?

Yes, I should

Not because I'm any more special than you

But simply because God told me I'm special in my own right

The crown has already been made for me

I know it is mine

So, for now, I am a king uncrowned

But my time is coming

And there is NO denying that

When you are trying to become something greater than what you currently are, you have to have a vision of the future. You have to have faith in not only what you can do for yourself, but how that higher power is going to help you achieve things you didn't even know were possible. So, you have to set goals, but you also have to have dreams.

There have been points when I thought dreamin' was pointless. Other times I felt like the word dream itself was an acronym standing for "does reality even actually matter." When I feel like that, my dreams tell me that sometimes "real life" is not what's most important. It is imperative to dream and live your life so that one day your dream will become your reality.

Then, you will be allowed to dream even bigger...

Dreamin'

I try to have dreams like King, Martin Luther, but pursue and they might shoot ya

Two-faced praisin' as they shoutin' "Hallelujah"

It's hot on the devil's doorstep, but they sayin' it's all cool bruh

Trying to scrub my soul clean and using the bible for my loofah

It was written there was nothing before God created

And if I was made in his likeness, then I can comprehend the hatred

See, I'll dodge your verbal bullets like I was in the matrix

Movin' towards the creator is what keeps me the safest

So, I live my life until it's time for me to go

Keep searchin' for a "yes" because I'm tired of hearing "no"

So, no weapon forged against me will ever halt the ability to prosper

Envision myself stable with a family, Grammy and a few Oscars

"Man, you can't do that!" That's the type of stuff I hear

Let's get one thing clear, God didn't give me the spirit of fear

So, with that being said, the ideas in my head

Will forever live on, while failure ends up dead

And uh, may that concept please rest in peace

Continue towards my goal, so I set my mind at ease

"Please allow Jacob to progress as he lives through lyrics

And when I feel low, can the words please lift my spirits?"

'Cause I know, I have had some really rough times

And the devil planted suicidal thoughts in my mind

So, I admit I pondered it and put a smile on his face

Questioning my purpose of life in the first place

And the worst case was, if I would let him win

I would've left my folks in agony and left my life in sin

If that would have happened, I couldn't see my father and grandparents again

Because taking the easy way out seems to be the trend

But I ain't ever really been a trendy-type dude

Tryin' to be like Big Mama and Goodie Mob, I want that soul food

And I told you before, I'm not like everyone else

I'll give my last to help others before I'll do for my self

Anyone who knows me can surely testify

And if anyone has issues, I always try to rectify

But I ain't never able to do quite enough

Keep lookin' in the sky, just so I can see what's up

And when I do, God gives me the strength to progress

Prophetically preaching my future while making satan upset

Yes! My mission will be accomplished

And thinking dreams can't become reality is just nonsense

I have aspirations, goals and dreams. It is not enough to just have them, but you have to also work to achieve them. Generally, the harder you work, the more likely you are to accomplish what you are trying to accomplish. Reaching one goal in particular has been incredibly difficult for me and that is... getting married.

I have always been a shy person. I've never been the type to like the spotlight being directly on me. Because of that I have moved away from solo opportunities in my music and my writing. My shyness has also caused issues with meeting and speaking to the young lady who is made for me; the one who will be my wife. My destiny is to find her so that we can build our future.

When that happens, our union will be a blessed one...

<u>**This Union**</u>

I remember the first time I actually saw her in person

I was thinking to myself, "She can't possibly be here to go out with me"

I had talked to her on the phone, so I had an idea of her personality

I had seen pictures of her, so I had an idea of what she looked like

But phone conversations and pictures did not do her justice at all!

Her looks were...well.... she certainly looked like she was out of my league

She didn't act like it, though

She was smiling from the moment we officially introduced ourselves and that

helped to eliminate the small amount of nervous energy I had

I felt comfortable with her from day one and that was something very new to me

It seemed as if we had known each other for years

I felt like I knew what she was looking for in life and it seemed like she knew

me as well

We were speaking without saying a word and I was astonished

And now...I can't believe how far we have come

I wasn't really nervous then, but now I am

I'm trying to stand still, but I'm rocking back and forth as I wait for "her music" to

start playing

And when it does...

I take a look back at my brother

I know he's waiting on me to start crying or something, but I am trying my best to

not do so

If for some reason a single tear comes out of my eye, I'll just have to blame it on my allergies or something

On second thought, I take that back

If the sight of my soulmate makes me shed a tear, then so be it

Then it started

The music that they played on those tv shows and movies is being heard by everyone as they all stand up in unison and look back at her

They are staring at the woman, who in a very short time, will officially become my wife

She is way beyond beautiful

The white dress she is wearing makes everyone focus on my angel

Ok, so now the emotions are starting to hit me

In my mind, I'm going back to that first night at the movies

I'm remembering how I couldn't focus on the film because I kept looking at her

Her smile gave me one of the best feelings I had ever felt in my life and now she was about to become my wife

Although she has a vail covering her face, I can see she is crying just a little more with each step she takes

I know they are tears of joy and they are affecting me greatly

The pastor she has been knowing since she was a teenager is performing the ceremony

When she reaches the alter, he reaches out for her hand and brings her to where I am

"She is really about to be my wife!"

My thoughts are kept to myself

I'm trying not to smile too hard, but I feel like I'm failing miserably

I know some people are thinking, "It's about time!"

Those type of thoughts don't upset me because I agree

It is indeed about time

Better yet, it's about timing

And for me to have this moment happen, the timing had to perfect

God had to see I was ready for her at the exact time she was ready for me

He had to see that we were both ready to become one

And since he did, here we stand

My hand is now shaking a little because I'm placing the wedding band on her

finger

Soon, she places the band on my finger

She lets out a slight sigh of relief because we have both finally made it to a place

we had been trying to get to for quite some time

Not just as a couple, but before we even knew each other

This is what we hoped for

This is what we prayed for

And now, we have it

"You may now kiss the bride."

I am no longer even trying to fight the smile as those six words are being said

I kiss her

No longer my girlfriend

No longer my fiancé

But my wife

The world will be able to see her as what I thought she was when I first met her...

My soulmate

God blessed us before we knew each other

He blessed us and allowed us to meet

He continued to bless us as we fought through our trying times together

"God, I know you are with us, I just ask that you continue to bless this union!"

Victory is an awesome thing! It doesn't matter whether your victory was when you finally found your soulmate - or when you finally get that promotion at work. What matters is how wonderful it is to look back at where you started and where you are (and where you plan to go).

I always think about what I'm trying to do in my life and ask myself what do I have to accomplish?

This is how I will know when I've "made it"...

We Made It

Victory is no longer a mystery

It is now a part of our future's history

Which means today is the day we set out to reach

Today we learn what others have set out to teach

We made it

I can't be stressed on the journey to success

Life will get messy, this has to be confessed

Anyone who's great has gone through those times

When they almost went crazy because of stress, they thought they'd lose their

minds

Some will say you've made it, even when you think you have a way to go

Some say you haven't learned what you already know

But a win will not be given, you have to go out and take it

An opportunity may not be presented, sometimes you'll have to make it

It's no secret... I want a family of my own. At the time of me writing this, it has not happened for me, but I KNOW things have already been put in place to change that. So, I'm not worried.

As a man, not only do you look forward to having the woman of your dreams by your side, but you also want to have a son. See, kids are a blessing and each one is special. However, when it comes to a son, you start talking about your legacy. You picture watching various sports games with him and hoping he ends up liking all of the same teams you do.

Maybe one day my son will get to read this book. Oh, what a day that will be

What's up, Son?

Seeing you is like seeing something I have imagined for quite some time

God certainly blessed your mother and I with you

Seeing your toothless smile for the first time... well, that's something that can't be described

And even though it would have been cool if your first word would have been "Dad" or something like that, hearing you start to express yourself was amazing

When you took your first steps, it seemed like you were in a hurry to go somewhere

I laugh because I can only imagine the plans you already had formulated in your head

Your mother says all the time that you act just like me

Now, as much as I like to hear that, that's both good and bad

It's good because it's like... through you, I'm getting a chance to see how my father felt when I was growing up

What it was like to see a younger version of someone very similar to who he was

Being able to compare baby pictures and seeing what features were like his

On the flip side of things, being like me means you also carry over some of my stubbornness

Some of my attitude issues

Some of my inability to hold back on how much truth you tell people (at times)

And the thing that got me in trouble a lot growing up was how I sometimes felt I had to let the slick, sarcastic comments leave my mouth...

Even though you're young, I can already see you have that trait as well

But I wouldn't trade any of it for anything

I thank your mom all of the time for bringing you into the world

I am so thankful for her, for you.... for my family

You all have made me wealthy beyond measure

As you grow older, I hope to see you like some of the things your mother and I do

I can't wait to go to one of your school concerts as you play in the band

Or go to one of your photo or art exhibits

I'm already proud and none of that has happened yet

As you get older, just know you have more power than you can imagine

Don't just follow what your friends do because you are a leader

Keep doing what you know is right, even when the people want to tell you

otherwise

I am proud of you everyday and I hope you know this

Also, don't think I haven't noticed how you treat your sister

No, I'm talking about when you two are arguing

That's more for attention

That's not really how you feel about her

I know you love her

I see you protecting her when you all are walking home from school

You put your arm around her and you won't let any harm come her way

I truly appreciate that

She acts like she can't stand you, but you know better

She adores you, just as your sibling, she just doesn't want you to know it

Continue to protect her because one day your mother and I won't be around

She needs you

No matter how old you two get, that will never change

You two have to be able to communicate with each other

Because one day, somebody will need the other to just listen as they vent

Son, you allow me to see a better version of myself and I thank you for that

No matter what, know that your father loves you

Having a daughter is a "different kind of special" than having a son (at least I feel it will be). For a woman, I'm sure they get all kinds of pride seeing their little girl act like them, just as we do when we have our sons. However, there is something special about a father's relationship with his little girl.

As a father, we are the first man our daughters get to see. Therefore, their opinions of men (good or bad) will start with us. If we do our job properly, our daughters will understand when a young man is not treating her the way she should be treated, and so many little princesses will be able to one day become someone's queen (like her mother is to me).

<u>**Daddy's Girl**</u>

My little girl

I can't express how happy your mother and I were to find out we were going to

have a daughter

Having a little girl forces all of us men to step up

From day one we always want you to stay away from men who have any faults

So we try not to have any ourselves

I remember when we all went into the store and you saw a ballerina tutu

It was so cute the way you smiled and were jumping up and down that you caught

the attention of a little boy who was with his mom

Your brother and I both noticed at the same time

It was funny how he stepped in front of you, looked at the little boy and just shook

his head to say "Stop looking at my sister!"

That's my boy!

That sort of thing just lets you know we all care, but the relationship between a

father and his daughter is special

I am how you start learning about how men are

You will compare how those in the future treat you with how I did

Just know, no matter what...

At first, I won't feel any guy is good enough for you

I know this will upset you, but it's still going to happen

Your mother is the queen and you certainly are my princess

As a princess, you deserve the best

So, forgive me in advance for always wanting that for you

One day you'll realize I meant well

I hope you learn to appreciate your brother

Sure, I know he gets on your nerves, but I hope you know he loves you

Sometimes us guys just have a crazy way of showing we care for someone

Look out for him the way he looked out for you

If that is done, you two will have no problems in this crazy world

He will run into women who he swears is the love of his life

You'll immediately know he is wrong, but know when it comes to love....

Many times us guys don't really know what's going on

Express your opinion to him, but don't make him feel idiotic for his decisions

You two mean the world to your mother and I

As you get older, just stay close

I don't care when if you're 40, to me you'll still be my little girl

And I love you

What does it take to actually say you've made it? How much do you have to have in life for you to be happy? Does a smile appear on your face because of materials or because of people? I'm asking all of that to ask, what is success?

In my life, some of the best things truly were the ones that were free, while some things that cost a lot ended up meaning nothing to me. So, does success come from money? To me, it partially does, but then again, not really. See, success is one of those words that has a formal definition, but that definition sometimes seems completely out of place. It's one of those things that an individual determines.

So, again I ask... what is success?

Success

Nobody can tell you what success is because it's different for each one of us

Sure, there may be an actual definition of the word, but that's not what I'm speaking of

One person can say you are not successful if you make less than $100,000 a year

What gives them that right, though?

If a person makes more than me, it doesn't mean they are successful, it just means they make more money than me

In my mind, success is being happy

Success is having people who love you

Success is doing the things you love to do and not fear trying new things

Knowing that even when you mess up, you have a chance to make up for it

That is success

Now, have I always been where I am now?

No

Am I currently where I want to be?

No, because there's always room for improvement

So, if all of these contradictions are true...

What is success?

It is simply what you want it to be and nothing more

Your success is not the same as mine and vice versa

My sadness is not yours

Your happiness may not necessarily be mine

So, there are many things that can be said about success

But nobody on this earth can tell you what that word means

And when you understand that, some might say you are already successful

I don't like to admit it, but we're all merely mortals. At some point, my journey will reach its end. What I did in my life will become not who I am, but who I was.

For some, those type of thoughts can be very depressing. For others, it just makes them think about how they live their lives on a daily basis.

No matter which way you look at it, death will come for us all...

The Death of Me

It was a day I knew I would get to, but one I didn't want to see

People who I hadn't seen in years were now standing and shouting about J.G.

Social gatherings are supposed to bring people glee

But things are a little different, for this is the death of me

Did I live long? Well, time is subjective, so that would be a matter of opinion

Did I sin? Of course, but I pray that I've been forgiven

My family is all crying, but I really wish they would not

For just as a life starts, one day it'll have to stop

The preacher is saying all positive things, feeling my family with pride

I was by no means perfect, but I pray God and the world knew I tried

I pray my family doesn't feel any pain just because I'm not here

I pray my memory gives them strength, instead of my absence giving them fear

I hope my wife knows I loved her with all of my heart and soul

I thank God for the time he gave me with her, it was worth far more to me than
any amount of gold

She helped me understand what love was, a life lesson I was happy to learn

It seemed I waited forever for happiness, but she showed it was well worth
waiting for my turn

I hope my kids know I loved them, too

I appreciate the good times and even the bad ones they put me through

I hope my son is able to surpass anything I was ever able to do

I pray he knows when he was younger, he would fall asleep as I said "Son, I'm proud of you!"

And as he grew up, I could see him getting closer and closer to his dreams

I look forward to him accepting his symbolic crown as one day, he becomes a king

And my daughter, well, what can I say?

Any man would be lucky to call her his wife someday

She has the looks of her mother, but with an even more modern twist

If they did a search for they perfect little girl, she would certainly be it

Both kids are creative like us and they have the intelligence to match

Just thinking I had anything to do with their creation....well, I can't be mad at that

I admit, it does sadden me that I will never again be able to give any of them a hug

But I hope they know they will forever have my love

God, I know it's over, but I want to thank you for all of the seconds

that added up to my life

Thank you for sharing the moments of those that passed before me,

my kids and my wife

Thank you for my father, mother, brother, other family members and my friends

I appreciate the beginning of my life, my progression and even how I

reached the end

It was a day I knew I would get to, but one I didn't want to see

I now bow out gracefully from this world, for this is the death of me

As I said before, we all have a story. The preceding was just a portion of mine. My World, My Words, my life, my dreams, my emotions, my thoughts, my past and vision of the future have all been put on display to give you The Book of Jacob.

As we go though life, we will all go through things that will make us feel like we're all alone. We'll convince ourselves nobody could possibly understand what we're going through, but this is 100% false. In reality, nobody actually has to go through heartache or pain alone. We, for whatever reason, choose to.

We forget God is always there, even when we can't seem to find anyone else who can handle us while we're dealing with our various issues. He can hear your heart when you have no words. He can feel your pain when you can't even understand what exactly has hurt you. If you trust Him when you're down, He most certainly will be able to lift you up!

Life isn't always bad, though. Even if a person (such as myself) has dealt with many bouts of depression and multiple thoughts of suicide, we have to have faith things will get better. If we believe that, then they will. They will have no choice. When we are able to fight through the lowest points of our lives, we will appreciate the high points much more.

Each day is another chance to make things better, not only for yourself, but for those you care about. Tell the people you love how important they are to you because, as sad as it is, one day you will not be able to. Cherish their presence because the present is truly a gift. Tomorrow is definitely not promised, but if you are fortunate enough to be blessed with today, please make the most of it.

Until the next book.....

Love & live life to the fullest!

Thank You

Wow! We've actually made it to the second book. It may have taken longer than I wanted and I know some people thought this would never happen, but here we are. Without wasting any more time, let me go ahead and thank those who have made this possible.

As with the last book release (and anything else in my life), it is absolutely necessary for me to thank God. A lot of things have happened since "My World, My Words" became available. Some of those things could have caused me to not only give up on writing, but to give up on life – fortunately, God didn't allow that to happen. This certainly would not have been possible without you. I am forever grateful. Thank you!

I would like to thank my mother for being a strong woman. She has shown a quiet strength that is astonishing! With a smile on her face, I have seen her take on things many people twice her size and half her age would struggle with. She has shown me that no matter the odds, you can overcome anything if you believe you can. To my brother, your level of focus far exceeds that of those way older than you. It certainly surpasses mine and I am not ashamed to admit that. It gives me something to aim for. Thank you. Also, I would like to thank my new sister-n-law, Logan Grovey (still have to get used to that). Thank you for being around to bring some additional happiness to my brother's life. Welcome to the family! Lastly, when it comes to immediate family, I would like to thank my father (to whom this book is dedicated). While it is true you are no longer with us physically, we still feel your presence. I know you're still around, even when others don't believe me. Words could never express how much influence you had on me, nor how much we miss you,

I have a lot of family members to thank and I just wanted to say, these are in no particular order, so I don't want anyone to get upset with me. To my aunt

Carolyn, I want to thank you for never being "fake." If you have an opinion on something, I'm glad you've always been willing to speak your mind. I also have to thank her kids (my cousins) Angela and Anthony. Angela, you, Lewis, Jordan and Brandon are just great people to be around. I appreciate the youthful spirit you all seem to always carry around. I don't think y'all realize how much that helps people. Anthony, you and your family (Johann, Logan and London) are like a real life version of the Huxtable family or something, at least to me. I also want you to know I appreciate you being able to bring humor to whatever situation you're in. The world needs to see more of you (hopefully we can get you a tv show or something one day).

To my cousin RB, I thank you for still being there to listen when I need to just ramble on about some of my dreams. I know you have a lot going on in your world, so just stay focused because the population needs to not only see you box, but they need to hear your music! So, make it happen! When you do, I know your wife and kids will be extremely proud of you! And my cousin Grovey, don't stop the hustle, man. I already know you'll be doing your thing, there's no doubt about that. Don't just strive for a million! I would also like to thank my aunt (and their mother) Donna Kay. I appreciate you and Charles being extremely hospitable to me whenever I'm in town. I also truly want to thank you for continuing to speak about my dad. I certainly appreciate you keeping his memory alive. I can't express enough gratitude for that. I also need to send a shout out to Darryl and Vaughn Jonson and Shaluan Douglas. Thank you!

If that weren't enough, I have more family that I have to thank. Danny, Yvonne and Ki... thank you. I appreciate y'all for not only being supportive of my work (both music and writing), but for staying true to who you are. When others (who shall remain nameless) have flip-flopped their personalities and opinions, y'all have not. When others have seemed to say one thing to my face, but something different when I'm not around, y'all have not. Life has changed since my dad passed and I thank y'all for helping the family make it through some emotionally difficult times.

The extended family I spoke about in the last book, well, they are still around. So, I would like to thank everyone again (but forgive me if a don't include a description as lengthly as I did in the first book). Danny and Eddie even though we don't talk as much, y'all are still my brothers and I don't take that for granted. Both of you know you can reach out to me whenever and I know that is reciprocated. Eddie, it makes me happy to see that you and Tiffany have been happily married for so long. Danny, I continue to thank you and Equasta for prayer during some of those very dark moments in my life. I wan't you all to know it's inspirational to see people you grew up with actually be "grown." Equasta I hope you keep that bubbly personality you have because it almost forces people to be happy. Chandra, thank you for always thinking about my best interest and letting me know your opinion (even when I didn't really seem too open to actually hear it). I'm grateful you've been around as long as you have. I appreciate that. Dominique, I'm proud of you little sister and the recent activities in your life. Keep moving forward! I'd also like to thank Angel. I know we don't talk much but it's good to know if I send out a random text, I'll hear back from you with some good advice.

Now, on to my extended Florida family. Karl, thank you for remaining the same over the years. You have always been a difficult person to get ahold of, but when I do reach you, I know I'm gonna have a positive conversation. Byron, I'm glad you're doing more with your music these days. Thank you for showing you can still pursue your dreams, even when you postpone them for a while. Skyler, I hope you know major moves are in store for your future! Thank you for helping me through some of my struggling times, especially in Cali. Brandon, thank you for finally working on more music! It's about time! Just playin'. Adaryll, whenever we are able to catch up with each other, you remind me that we all have talent and even when it seems like we haven't done anything, we actually have. Collectively,

I will say the people I just mentioned could pick up their phones more often (but I'm not calling you out or anything).

There are a few more people that I most certainly have to thank. To Miranda, I thank you for being a part of these various projects over the years. I promise you will make it! And just like in the last book, I have to thank Amber, but also remind her she is still too young to be seriously thinking about boys and dating (at least in my opinion, lol). Ketrina and Fred, I still thank you for being yourselves. Trina still has the ability to not talk to a person for a year, then yell at them as if they just talked yesterday. Keep it up! Fred, thanks for the conversations that would start with phrases like, "Listen young brother...." and would be followed by necessary advice. I also need to thank John for giving me a reason to finally see a part of the world I had always dreamt of! Your wedding was awesome, man and I know you and Jane will be happy! Seeing Africa was most certainly full of inspirational moments that will remain with me for the rest of my life. AB, thank you for still being around. We've helped each other deal with some difficult times and I appreciate it. Debraca, I thank you for still being cool and jokingly providing me with the title for this book! Who knows what it would have been called had it not been for you? To the homie, Jermaine: thank you for believing in my work over the years. That certainly doesn't go without notice. It's also necessary for me to thank Koko. 'Preciate you, player. YBR, R4L (inside info). Stay positive because people really need that type of energy around them! There are many great things in store for your future and I pray you are ready for it all! Please, never doubt your abilities or your potential.

I must also take a moment to thank those who were a part of my life, but God has called them home. Big Mama and Grandpa, we all still miss y'all everyday. There isn't a family gathering that goes by where you won't hear somebody quoting y'all. Maurice, Elza , "Jr." Frederick and Angela: don't ever think we have forgotten about y'all because we haven't. Also, once again, I would like to thank my father. It's amazing to hear how often people say I act like you, but I guess you knew we acted alike all along. We truly miss you all and you will always be with us.

When I was nearly finished with this book, I decided to start a Kickstarter campaign to try to help out with some of the funding. I had never attempted a campaign before, but I had faith things would work out. So, I would like to individually thank everyone who donated the amount that included being a part of this section as one of the rewards. Some of the following names are listed above, but they needed to be recognized again. Skyler Brumm, Grovey Latimer, John Mwangi, Jewels Phillips, Joey Ricard and Debraca Russell. If that weren't enough, there was also Ashley Briscoe, Janice Grovey, Dwayne Griffeth, Greg Grovey, II and Jim Leggat. The list continues with Dustin Gierst, Matt Parker, Korenn Lenny, Sophia Preston, Chandra and Nathan Lott and Jacqulyne Allmon, Joshua Bing, Daniel and Equasta White, Adaryll Horne, David McKenzie and Nick Slater along with countless others who made other contributions, posted the link to my page on twitter, facebook and helped spread the word by just telling others. I am very grateful for everyone's efforts and you all deserve recognition for helping to make one of my dreams a reality.

To all of the readers, I would be remiss if I didn't thank you. I truly, truly appreciate you taking the time to view the words I have put on paper to express how I feel (and have felt) about my life. I hope you were able to find something in this book that you will take to heart and pass along to other people. Thank you!

Everyone has impacted my life differently, but all of the impact is important. Who I am would be different if you weren't who you are. So, I thank you all. Again, I know I have forgotten people and I apologize if you were not mentioned. I value you and all that you have done, but sometimes the mind can't remember the same things the heart can.

www.ingramcontent.com/pod-product-compliance
Lightning Source LLC
Chambersburg PA
CBHW070446120726
47910CB00003B/943